A WALK THROUGH THE MIND

THE MIND

VOLUME ONE:

HUDDERSFIELD AUTHORS' CIRCLE

SOPHIE ALDERHEART   GEMMA ALLEN

SARA BURGESS   GARETH CLEGG   KATH CROFT

SUSIE FIELD   NICK STEAD   VIVIEN TEASDALE

OWEN TOWNEND

COPYRIGHT

INTRODUCTION

Take a walk with us, through our thoughts, our feelings, our hopes and our dreams. Wander through the darkness that hides behind the light of the soul. Take a walk with the authors of the Huddersfield Authors' Circle and be swept away in the poetry and prose within these pages.

These literary pieces are the accumulated work of our group through competitions held by our President and external adjudicators. It is the second book produced by the Circle, and it has been made with our very own blood, sweat and tears.

The last few years have been difficult for us all and throughout it, our writers have powered through and brought their all to our workshops, meetings and competitions.

This book is a testament to that eternal struggle we face as writers to get our voices out into the world.

**So sit back and relax while you
take a walk through our minds.**

DEDICATED TO:

John Emms 1949-2021
A great scriptwriter and an inspiration to us all.
Thanks for all the joy you brought to the Circle.
You'll be sadly missed.

CONTENTS

WATER - 2018

PRESIDENT'S COMPETITION

A POINTED SOLUTION

OWEN TOWNEND

Mel bustles into work, knife concealed in the left sleeve of her red quilted jacket. The inner seam is already soaked with Chaudelot's blood, so this will be the last time she wears it. Fortunately there is another in the wardrobe at home in case anyone gets suspicious. It belongs to her sister and Mel would rather not 'borrow' any more from her than she already has.

There are no hold-ups at the main entrance: a swift sign-in and small talk with Barton the Guard. However, once Mel is through the security gate, William from Marketing ambushes her. He is wearing his black toupee, out to impress the younger man beside him who is casually-dressed in a blue shirt with an open collar.

"Mel," William says, glancing at his watch. "Long lunch?"

"Something like that."

He locks eyes with her but soon loses interest.

"This is Ryan Sharry, the latest addition to our first-floor team. I'm just giving him the full building tour. Ryan, this is

Mel Varley. She's up-and-coming in Public Relations, one of our best." William winks.

"Nice to meet you," Ryan Sharry says, holding out a hand.

Mel reaches out with her left instinctively but stops herself before the knife comes loose. Noticing William and Ryan's confused stare, she feigns wrist pain.

"Sorry," she says. "RSI."

William frowns. "Don't you have an ergonomic keyboard?"

"Hardware trouble." Mel says, offering her right hand. Ryan shakes it, his eyebrow still raised. "My apologies, Ryan. It is great to meet you. I just have to run to the kitchen for something."

"Everything all right?"

"Yes, just gasping for a glass of water."

"Another migraine coming on?" William asks.

"Possibly. I'll have my water then sit down in the dark for a while. Please excuse me."

Mel slips past them with what she hopes resembles her usual easy smile. Ryan glances back at her in bemusement till William steers him towards Barton's desk.

As soon as Mel reaches an empty hallway, she lets the smile drop and sprints to the communal kitchen. It is expansive with squat white plastic cupboards and black granite countertops. She checks that the alcove seating area is empty before finally locking the kitchen door.

Searching the cupboard, she chooses a tall glass right at the back. It has dust on the rim but she doesn't bother rinsing, just turns to the tap and fills the tumbler to the top with cold water.

With one final glance around, she takes out the knife. It is made of a thin translucent plastic, the edge dulled after the stabbing. Nevertheless, there are still some flecks of blood on the blade so she rinses this under the tap. Then when the knife is as clean as it's going to be, Mel drops it into the glass.

The plastic knife fizzes loudly as it dissolves. Her sister warned about this: that the experimental polymer, while definitely water-soluble, still has some reactive issues. Mel gently shakes the glass to make sure that the blade fully breaks down and that there are no bits left to settle at the bottom.

She really doesn't know enough about this to be sure it will work. When she swiped the polymer from her sister's home lab, it was in the hope that it would prove as undetectable as promised.

As for the killing, Chaudelot brought it on himself. Blackmail is a risky business, especially when you go after someone like Mr Scaife. It didn't matter that there was irrefutable footage of a dodgy deal, he would retaliate accordingly. He used one of his more morally-flexible employees to handle the deed and wipe the records clean. After all, why would Mr Scaife want to get his hands any dirtier than they already were?

The first time he asked Mel to sort out such a problem, he had summoned her to his office, asked personally, proposed a raise. This time it had merely been a cursory phone call that had lasted less than a minute. While he had forgotten his manners, she had gone ahead and put in more effort into covering both their tracks. How is that fair?

If she is honest with herself, it isn't. Scaife thought he could just say a few words and she would put herself in harm's way simply for the sake of job security. Typical man, thinking his charm is limitless. Another raise is in her future, whether he likes it or not.

Mel snatches the glass from the countertop and shakes it again. She holds the bottom up to the light, searching for any telltale clumps. Turning back to the kitchen door, she glimpses Trudy, Mr Scaife's PA, staring incredulously. Mel holds up an apologetic hand and lets her in.

"What the hell?" Trudy asks, adjusting her glasses.

"Sorry," Mel replies. "I needed a moment."

Trudy tilts her head, frowning sympathetically. "Another migraine?"

"A small one." Mel lays the glass back down on the countertop. "I think it's passed."

Trudy nods and points at the tumbler. "Have you drunk from that yet?"

"No. Why?"

Trudy rolls her eyes. "It's Mr Scaife. He's come downstairs to give the new guy the big company welcome. His throat's getting a bit dry."

Mel glances at the glass. Her sister had said that the polymer would dissolve completely, given time. Presumably, if there are no plastic bits left at the bottom, the water will be fine to drink. Or not. It is an experimental polymer, after all. She has taken a risk with Mr Scaife so now it seems fitting for him to take a risk with her.

She hands Trudy the glass of water. "Make sure he takes big sips..."

AQUA PURA

VIVIEN TEASDALE

Tear
by tear
cupped hands
catch at splashes.
Cleanse calloused fingers,
washing away long morning
treks across the lands that stained their
lives with untold sorrows. Now they
dance, life overflowing with elation,
tomorrow transformed,
because water is just
the beginning

ARK—ZERO—NINE

GARETH CLEGG

They were all dead. All of them, except Yanik.

Yanik was small for his age, even in these difficult times when everyone was skinny. Food was sparse, and much of it was too poisonous to eat without processing. He stood barely four feet in height when all the other kids of his age towered over a foot above him; always looking down, always teasing, relentless, unless one of the Elders intervened.

His mother had named him Yanik, but by his third year, everyone could see he was different, a runt, and that's what they called him. Runt, Squat, Shorty, Short Arse - they were terribly inventive with their names. Even the adults used those names for him, except Jaydn.

Jaydn had looked after Yanik when his mother died. They hadn't thought the five-year-old boy could understand what had happened, but Yanik knew it was his fault. He was the one who had brought the water to her, not realising it was from the Black River, that it carried the invisible blight in each cool, refreshing mouthful.

She hadn't died straight away. The slow and painful

process had taken weeks as his mother's body fell apart. First, she had been sickly and weak, vomiting and unable to eat. Later, her hair began falling out in clumps, and finally, bloody bruises started to grow all over her body.

She bruised and bled from the slightest pressure, so much so that she couldn't bear to be touched. He still couldn't imagine the pain she must have endured and hidden from him. The last time he saw her she smiled, hugged and kissed him and then told him to go with Jaydn. He somehow knew he wouldn't see her again and Jaydn had been forced to carry him out, kicking and screaming.

That had been ten years ago. He still felt the anguish of not being there for her at the end, but at fifteen Yanik was almost a grown man. The irony wasn't lost on him; he was often reminded of his childlike stature by the children and adults alike.

All the children of his age were expected to work and contribute to the clan. Though most did it with petulance, Yanik seemed to instinctively understand the need. It was their duty to make the world a better place, safer for the rest of the clan.

A sharp crack of stone on stone snapped Yanik's mind back into sharp focus, and the danger he still faced. He and his crew had been scavenging for essential raw materials and scrap that could be transformed, by people such as Jaydn, into useful items, indispensable items in some cases.

Hushed conversation reached his ears, along with sounds of movement approaching. A dull beam of light cut through the inky darkness, illuminating the entrance of the crevice he had wedged himself into. He wanted to squirm further back into the claustrophobic debris-strewn hiding place but feared that the slightest of sounds would draw the attention of his pursuers. Holding his hand across his mouth, Yanik tried to breathe, slow and shallow.

The rubble from the collapsed building walls dug into the exposed flesh of his arms and lower legs. Something sharp was agony in his left hip, probably some of that metal that was inside the stone the ancients used to construct their larger buildings. Yanik couldn't risk moving and bit his index finger to try and take his mind from the gouging pressure in his side.

Scree and rubble shifted outside the hiding place. The light wavered, trying to crawl its way further up the narrow crevice to paint his face with a dull yellow glow. That would be the end of him.

"What's you up to, Ravos?" a rough accented voice cut through the silence from further away.

"Thought I heard somethings," the reply was much closer, the one with the light, "Nah, too small, must be rats."

"Rats is good eating. We should have a poke about and see if we can gets us some suppers."

"No time. One of those little shitters got away. Needs to catch it before they can finds friends and bring thems back here."

The low grumbling from the one further away and the dimming of the light gave Yanik hope. It was only then he realised he'd been holding his breath. He let it out into his palm, desperate to keep the sound from passing any further towards the waiting ears of the raiders outside.

Though Yanik hated the teasing and bullying about his size, today he was relieved that he was small enough to crawl into this tiny gap between the collapsed buildings and rubble.

He waited unmoving for what seemed an eternity in the consuming darkness.

Yanik's head jerked and he cursed. "Shit, can't afford to fall asleep here." In the all-consuming darkness, it was difficult to establish how long he had been sleeping. The pain in his hip was raw and had been joined by cramp settling into his calf muscles. It made him want to scream and stretch, but he waited silently in his rocky tomb.

Hearing nothing, and with the pain becoming unbearable, he made his move, slowly pushing away from the metallic object digging into him. He stretched his calf muscles, trying to get feeling back into them.

Even though he moved slowly and carefully, there were scrapes of stone as his body dislodged small rocks and scree which had settled beneath him. The sounds were like a siren blaring into the deathly silence around him, announcing his location to the killers in the dark.

He expected running boots and torchlight outlining him in the blackness, but all remained silent in the enveloping darkness. He should be more careful. It was lack of care that had been the end of the other three members of his crew - Tyler, Kallid and Ruba.

Ruba had been the best of them. She hadn't liked him, but at least she understood the importance of what he knew and contributed. She'd tried to keep Tyler and Kallid off his back, well most of the time.

The two larger boys had been BloodSpears, warrior caste. They spent all their time fighting and training. They both hated Yanik and everything he stood for. They couldn't accept that someone small and weak like him was of any use to the clan. The Elders revered his skills above those of the warriors, and the BloodSpears didn't like that at all.

Yanik was, after all, much more than just a scavenger.

His uncle had passed on every ounce of skill and lore of the technology of the ancients. Yanik was as good as anyone in the clan at taking those long-lost materials and crafting things of great value. People like him kept the old machines working, the pumps and filters that provided potable water, so they no longer had to rely on testing and decontaminating every drop. They repaired the tools and weapons their clan relied on to produce enough food to feed them all and to protect them from the raiders and slavers who would try and steal it all from them.

Ruba was—had been—a Teller. They kept the knowledge and history of the clan, along with responsibility for the religious rites of birth, marriage and death. They were the ones responsible for recording, interpreting, and enforcing the laws and teachings of Leviathan.

Yanik hadn't been friends with Ruba, hell he wasn't friends with anyone, except Jaydn, but that was different. Jaydn was like a father to him; well in reality, an uncle.

His small fingers clawed at the crevice exit; even he had to squeeze his tiny frame out of the narrow gap. A sobering thought struck him. *Oh, these better have just been raiders and not flesh-eaters, by Leviathan let it be so.* It was hard enough imagining checking the corpses of his three dead crew members for any valuable items that might have been overlooked, without the thought of...

He gagged, but managed to steer his imagination away from those sorts of images, thrusting them into the depths of his subconscious. Instead, he reached down for the torch on his belt. Three rapid spins of its winder caused a horrendous whirring scream. He remained crouched in the darkness, straining to hear any signs that he might have been heard. After what seemed minutes, satisfied he was alone, he turned the torch on with a soft click. With the bright beam of white light playing across the rubble-strewn floor, he started picking his way back to where they had camped.

It had taken Yanik three days to drag Ruba back to the settlement once he had realised she was still alive. Her body had been a blood-soaked ruin with limbs twisted at unusual angles, unpleasant to even look upon, but he'd noticed the shallowest of breaths. Using his rudimentary medical knowledge, he did what he could for her before dragging her on their arduous journey back down the dark broken stairs and rubble-filled corridors.

Now, he waited with the rest of the clan as the bodies of the two BloodSpears, Tyler and Kallid, recovered by their clan-brothers, were carried through the crowded area by their kin. Wrapped in mushroom leather shrouds, which had already been stitched up to the chest, they were laid on the metallic floor at the edge of the enormous central shaft.

As Yanik stood in silence, watching the solemn crowd, he saw Jaydn making his way through them. Like a bubble through oil, they parted around him. He was a large man, bulky and tall. His thicket of hair and beard had been black as night when he had first arrived in the village, but the years had painted him with flecks of silver grey.

He moved purposefully to the bodies and laid a small bag down beside them.

Yanik had to push and squeeze between people as he struggled to make his way through to his uncle's side to kneel beside him. Opening the grey bag revealed the needles and cord to finalise the job of preparing the bodies for the afterlife.

Jaydn looked on approvingly as Yanik took the large needle from the bag and threaded the thick cord from the chest of the first shroud. Donning a single leather glove, he began the work of stitching it closed for its final journey.

The needle flew through the dense material under his direction. He alternated three stitches with pulling the cord tight, ensuring the stones that weighted the feet of the shroud would remain within, drawing it down into the depths and reunion with mighty Leviathan.

He paused as he reached the final stitch, then plunged the needle into the shroud and through Kallid's nose. The cartilage protested for a brief moment but couldn't resist the pressure the needle exerted.

Several of the onlookers winced, audible intakes of breath from a few near the front, but Jaydn's whispered words reassured him.

"That's it, lad. Last stitch through the nose, that's the law of the sea. If that doesn't wake him, then we know he's truly dead."

Yanik finished, tying off the cord with the knot Jaydn had taught him and cut the excess with his knife.

As soon as he completed the stitching on Tyler's shroud, the BloodSpears rushed in, almost knocking Yanik over. They lifted their clan-brothers, feet first, to the wooden trellis tables that edged the cylindrical shaft.

A hush descended over the assembled crowd as the Great Teller raised his wizened hands for silence.

"Unto almighty Leviathan we commend the souls of our brothers departed. We commit their bodies to the deep; in sure and certain hope of their resurrection unto eternal life.

Let their water mix with the mighty ocean depths, through our Lord, Leviathan."

As the crowd repeated "Leviathan," the wooden boards were raised. The leather-shrouded corpses plummeted into the yawning void, commencing their final journey to the rolling ocean waves far below.

DYING FOR A DRINK

NICK STEAD

Paul awoke to pain's hammer thundering within his skull, each blow striking a fresh ache in his vulnerable brain. A feeling of nausea ebbed and flowed through his gut, briefly receding only to return ever stronger at the crest of each new wave. He fought to keep the foul liquid from rising up his gullet while he lay there with his eyes firmly shut, wanting nothing more than to return to his drunken coma. But sleep's soothing arms refused to envelop him, and his discomfort only grew.

He was vaguely aware he wasn't in his own bed, his body registering the bouncy feel of an inflatable mattress. The sun was unusually warm on his face and there was a gentle rocking sensation, accompanied by the sound of some fluid lapping at the sides of the airbed. None of that seemed particularly important for the time being though, a single thought taking hold at the forefront of Paul's mind. Water. He needed water to counteract the beer and rehydrate.

Eyes still closed, he groped around on either side of him for the glass of H_2O he usually had the sense to keep nearby after a night of drinking, whether at home or a friend's. But his search was to no avail – his hand found only thin air. So he finally allowed his eyelids to part, confusion reigning at the sight awaiting him.

It seemed he'd never made it to anyone's house before he'd passed out, the sun blazing overhead like a sadistic god, its light far too intense for his current state. Paul turned his head to one side, frowning at the brightly coloured rubber filling his vision. It took him a moment to piece together what was happening, but once the few memories not completely obliterated by the alcohol came back, he reached a terrifying conclusion.

Praying he was wrong, Paul sat up and struggled with a fresh wave of nausea, not so much from the hangover now but in response to the fear awoken in him. His prayers went unanswered, the deep blue of the open ocean stretching out in every direction for as far as his eyes could see. The airbed was not an airbed at all but a liferaft drifting on the surface, a mere speck lost in the sheer vastness of the watery expanse. No land was visible on the horizon, no ships or aircraft in the immediate vicinity for him to attempt to flag down. He was utterly alone in this death sentence he'd been handed, short as it would surely be without that essential fluid he craved so.

The terror of the situation became too much and he lost his battle with his treacherous gut, leaning over the side to retch and heave the contents of his stomach until it was as empty as his current surroundings seemed to be. But of course the sea was far from empty, the apparent lack of life deceptive. And as if to remind him of that fact, something swam a little too close for comfort, close enough for him to catch a glimpse of the dark shadow just beneath the waves, yet far enough from the raft for its identity to remain hidden.

Alarmed, Paul retreated back within the rubber walls of his makeshift sanctuary, keeping his eyes fixed on the area where he'd seen the creature. It was then that he saw the dorsal fin break the surface, and he felt himself go cold. He'd heard people say how rare shark attacks actually were, but he'd also seen enough videos to know how quick the fearsome predators were to bite anything that took their interest. And he was horribly aware of what those teeth would do to the rubber raft, and then to his flesh.

The fin submerged but he could just make out the shape of the big fish lurking beneath the waves until it disappeared completely, back into the deeps. Yet still he remained on edge for some time after, half expecting it to launch a surprise attack from below. No attack was forthcoming, and eventually he forgot the shark, his thirst taking over once more.

Paul couldn't help but think longingly of the supply of fresh water aboard his mate's boat. His mouth felt unnaturally dry, his tongue sticking to its floor like a beached whale, his buds still coated in the unwholesome taste of the vomit. Swallowing was painful and did nothing to ease his equally parched throat, and the longer he sat there suffering, the greater the temptation became to take a sip of seawater to soothe his desiccating insides. The sound of it splashing with the movement of the tide was almost more than he could bear, and it took all his willpower to keep himself from having a drink.

Part of him wondered just what had happened in that blackout period between waking and drinking on board Marco's boat. Had something happened to the vessel which had called for an emergency evacuation onto the liferaft? But then, why was Marco not with him? He found himself facing the morbid possibility that his mate may well have been claimed by the ocean already, though that was perhaps a blessing under the circumstances. At least his friend would not have to endure the same long hours of torment Paul himself faced before the end came, and after all the beer, Marco probably hadn't even been aware of what was happening. His passing may well have been made peaceful by his drunken state, a small mercy granted by an otherwise grim fate.

The day wore on and the sound of the waves became too much. Paul found himself leaning back over the side, lowering his hands to the seawater to cup just enough for a sip of the fluid to wet his mouth, bad for him though it was. But just as his fingers dipped beneath the surface, his eyes picked up the return of the dark shadow rising from below, and he pulled back with a cry, watching in horror as the shark's head poked above the waves, maw agape with hunger.

He looked into black eyes as empty as the very abyss it surely came from, born of a darkness even sunlight couldn't touch in the deepest depths of the ocean. Perhaps such a place could even be the gateway to Hell, for where else could spawn something so savage and ruthless?

The shark remained on the surface for some time, head above the water and jaws gaping with every pass it made. Paul expected it to clamp down on the rubber at any moment with its row upon row of sharp teeth which promised nothing but a painful and bloody end. But again it surprised him by retreating to the depths once more, without taking so much as a test bite. Still, its return had shaken him more than the first encounter and his heart continued to pound long after the creature disappeared. Not even the new discomfort of the night's chill creeping into the air could distract him from the fear the creature invoked, and sleep continued to elude him.

He must have nodded off at some point once darkness fell, because he woke to find he was no longer alone. Shock sent his heart racing anew when he laid eyes on the man sitting across from him, the moon providing just enough light to recognise those familiar features.

"Marco?"

"Miss me?" his friend smirked, apparently undaunted by the sheer hopelessness of their situation.

"You bastard, what the fuck were you playing at leaving me out here all alone?"

Marco shrugged. "Chill, man, it's not like I abandoned you to your fate. I'm here now, aren't I? Facing the exact same end as you."

Paul's sluggish brain struggled to make sense of the situation, lack of both sleep and water making the answer harder to grasp. But finally it came to him.

"Oh God, I'm hallucinating!"

"Does it matter? Better to have some company than die alone, right?"

"Wrong. Fuck off; I'm going back to sleep."

When Paul next awoke, it was to discover he had made it through the night, though he wasn't very optimistic about his chances of surviving another if he didn't get a drink soon. He didn't even know if he could make it through the day, his body's craving for fluid worse than ever.

Marco was gone but the shark was back, gliding effortlessly beside the raft. He vaguely wondered if it was really the same shark he kept seeing and whether this was normal shark behaviour. He was no expert but it seemed odd for it to keep coming so close without taking a curious bite out of the object that apparently fascinated it so. And even if it had been a different shark each time, he felt sure at least one of them should have attacked.

As he thought about the strangeness of it all, he began to wonder if the shark was really the Grim Reaper stalking him in the shape of the ocean's most feared predator. Death takes many forms after all, and his own death could not be far off now. Perhaps the Reaper was waiting patiently for the dehydration to take its toll, waiting for Paul to slip away so he could finally sink his teeth in and drag his soul down to its watery grave. Or was Paul merely letting his imagination get the better of him? Staring again into those eyes filled with the darkness of the void, he wasn't so sure.

Another thought occurred to him. There were a few supplies that came with the liferaft plus one or two bits and pieces Marco had stored with it, including a fishing knife. His fingers gripped the hilt like it was his last lifeline as he raised the blade ready to strike, waiting for his moment before bringing it down in a fierce arc aimed at the creature's head. But the shark veered away as if it had sensed the attack coming, the metal missing its mark and slicing into the animal's side, spilling blood but dealing no more than what looked to be a minor flesh wound. The doomed man sat back in defeat, his attempt to thwart Death failed. Perhaps if he'd succeeded in killing the shark and could stomach its meat, it might have provided some moisture and enough sustenance to keep him going just long enough to be rescued. Or maybe it had been a false hope from the start. Either way, the fish had gone again, giving no second chances.

The ocean was beginning to feel endless, the hours stretching over what had surely been years. Paul had finally resigned himself to his fate, dejected and forlorn as he stared out across the waves with the same despondent eyes as a prisoner on death row. He saw the chunk of what was once a boat floating by with a glass of fresh water just sitting atop it, but it took his brain several moments to register what he was actually seeing.

"Careful, mate," Marco said, back beside him. "If I'm a hallucination, how can you be sure the glass of water is real?"

"It has to be," he croaked, eyes still fixed on his prize. He dove from the raft before his friend could say anything more and swam towards his last hope at salvation.

Marco was ahead now, the back of his head bobbing up and down just in front of the wreckage. Paul watched him turn as he closed in, and it was only then he noticed the gash on his mate's neck. Black eyes met his own and he was flashed a toothy grin. And finally, the shark attacked.

PENANCE

VIVIEN TEASDALE

'Give me the cup! I have earned it.'

The old man looked down at Barric and sighed.

'You are here, which means you have a right to the cup, but you have not yet earned it. You have much to learn before you make the final decision. Now tell me of your journey.'

'What journey? I've been nowhere, done nothing. Just give me the cup and let's get this over with.' Barric reached out to snatch the cup. The man in front of him was ancient, round and hunched up, shrivelled like some forgotten potato found at the bottom of the box when all else had been eaten. His clothes had the same mottled, grey-brown tiredness, but Barric's arm was held in a lightning-fast clamp and he was pushed back, away from the dais.

'You have done much but learned nothing. Now is your time to learn. Tell me of your journey, from the beginning when you were in the womb with your brother.'

'How can anyone remember that, fool? We were in the womb, he took up my space, the nourishment meant for me.'

'You weighed more than him when you were born.'

Barric hesitated. 'If you know that, you don't need—'

'I need you to tell me the truth. What happened to your brother?'

'He was just my brother. We grew up, squabbled like brothers do. Same as I squabbled withmy sisters, my cousins. We were that sort of family. So what?'

'How did he die?'

'We all played together. When the village had gatherings, it was always our family who provided the meats, the best players, the best runners.'

'And you were one of the best athletes, too. One of the best archers, the best wrestlers. What happened on your fifteenth birthday?'

'I was fifteen, I came of age. I was sent to Lord Godwin's to train as one of his guards. I was respected.'

'And Wymond? He stayed at home, yet he was the eldest. He should have—

'He should have ... been braver, been stronger. He wasn't, I was.'

'How did he die?'

'He was well when I left. I never saw him again.'

'Tell me of your life after you left the village.'

'I had to leave my home. Despite being the younger twin, I was to take my brother's place in the Palace Guards. With war looming in the North, Lord Godwin needed strong warriors around him and I was chosen. Proud, and yet ... angry at Wymond's easy acceptance of my taking his place, I marched away with Godwin between two of his guards, who showed me the best way to march easy, to catch the conies and make a quick meal over a campfire and how to build a shelter from the night winds and morning dew. I learned fast, earning my place in the company, respected by my fellow soldiers. My father visited, once, to see my passing out parade and watch us all leave for the noise and confusion of battle. We melded into a compact unit, the elite, the invincible, and I became their leader.

War suited me. As the horns sounded I could feel my blood rising, filling my heart, my mind and my eyes until everything I saw was outlined in the red of spilt blood. I felt nothing, heard nothing but the cries of my battlemates and the screams of my enemies. No-one stood before me, and even my friends knew to keep on the right side of me when in my battle frenzy. I crossed the great river, long the northern boundary of Lord Godwin's lands, and led his warriors deep into the territory of his cousin, taking the impregnable castle that had been Prince Haelan's stronghold. My lord became Prince over both lands and I his trusted war leader.

'And then I saw Alienor. She was my ideal, my perfection, my love. Her father accepted the price I offered and Prince Godwin gave me lands. I wanted for nothing and neither did she. Anything she asked for, she had. I loved her with a love that endured anything, that will endure forever, until eternity. But life moves on. I had to fight for my Prince. I came home wearied of battle and she healed my wounds, restored my soul. I lost my battle will, though still I led my soldiers into battle. I'd lost my blood lust and no-one but she knew.

'The north rebelled and I was sent to quell it. We burned the land, slaughtered the men, the youths just turning to manhood, the old and the young, even the babies. We destroyed the farms and drove the rest into the mountains to live as best they could in the desolate land. Those who survived the war, perished in the winter that followed. The northern tribes dwindled, though pockets lived on to lay claim to their fathers' lands.

'And I returned home, saddened by the needless deaths, the cutting off of young lives. I needed solace, a haven from my thoughts. I found none. Alienor was dead.'

The old man stirred at this. 'She was dead when you returned? How?'

'She died of a fever, a fever of the brain that took her reason. She knew not what she was doing. Her blood was let, as doctors always do, but too much was spilled and she perished.' Barric stared down at the bare ground, unwilling to let the old man see the tears in his eyes. Drop by drop they fell on the earth, and tiny shoots of grass slowly pushed their way up between and around his feet. Startled, he looked up.

'You feel remorse, Barric. You truly loved Alienor, then?'

'Oh, yes. She could have had anything from me, anything at all.

'Except her freedom? You wouldn't give her that, would you?'

'Why? Why are you torturing me like this?' Barric cried. 'You already know—

'But you haven't accepted it. You must know the depths of your soul before you can make your choice.'

'What choice?'

'Tell me everything and I will answer you. What happened in the graveyard? Your brother—'

'I loved him! How could I do otherwise? He was my twin, my other soul.' Barric fell to his knees, sobbing. 'He was my beloved,' he whispered.

'You were jealous of him.

Barric shook with fear, with anger, trying to control his thoughts. 'It was summer,' he croaked, 'he dared me to stay in the graveyard all night. I stayed; he ran away. And fell.'

'Tell me again.' The old man's eyes bore into him like spiky pieces of ice, and Barric could no longer control his words.

'As I fell, he ran to help me, hauling me up and consoling my fears. I pushed him away in anger. He was always better than me, a better hunter, better warrior, better son. How could I compete with him? And then he was there, helping me. He staggered back, falling hard against a jagged stone. His hip broke and Wymond never walked straight again, never rode easily, never fought in combat as a warlord should.'

'That is why you were sent to Lord Godwin? To take the place that rightfully belonged to your brother?'

'Yes. "Say nothing," Wymond told me, "it's between you and me. Just keep our secret and father will honour you with my training." He knew that was what I coveted above all else. And so I did what he said.'

'And then what?'

'It all happened just as I said. I became—'

'Yes, a great warrior and warlord, as you said. But what of the ending? What of Alienor?

Barric prostrated himself before the old man. 'I cannot,' he gasped. 'I cannot bear it. To live it again, it is too much.'

He was silent, clutching his grief to himself as it coursed through him, wracking his body and brain. The old man said nothing.

'She betrayed me.' Barric moaned. 'I came home to find her with another. In our own bed, in our marriage bed and she was with her lover. I needed respite from war and killing and blood, and she robbed me of everything I held dear. I still had my weapons on me. I don't know how, all I remember the screaming, her screaming, my screaming, his screaming. My sword plunging into her heart as she lay on the bed, stabbing down, through her, into his heart too and the blood spurting out, drenching us, painting us like the pagan warriors of old. And then my dagger was in my hand, plunging it into their throats, one after the other, and then into mine. I collapsed there, and we lay together, arms around each other, my wife, my brother and me. Inseparable.'

The old man sighed. 'You have learned enough of yourself, Barric. Now you can fulfil your journey. But you must listen yet awhile. Take the cup. Follow the road until you reach the river. There is a ford. It flows fast but is not deep. As the current flows down, it brings all your memories, all your mistakes, all your hatred, all your love. As it runs to the sea, it takes away all your memories, the good and the bad.

'You dealt death to many. You prized not even your own life. Now you must atone by living again, another life, a different life, to expiate your crimes.'

'Will I see them again? My ... my family?'

'Perhaps, perhaps not. The same applies to your friends, your enemies, to all mankind. But there is a choice. For everyone. Drink from whichever side of the river you wish. The flow from its source will allow you to keep all your memories in your next life, the other side will wipe the memories away, forcing you to start afresh. But remember, whatever you choose, it is for all eternity.'

Barric took the cup, glanced one last time at the sorrowing eyes of the old man and turned away towards the river.

THE HAT

SARA BURGESS

The house on Summerscale Lane is boarded up, set back from the main road behind a rusty gate that was once grand. Its garden is overgrown, the path is cracked, and the roof looks sad, as if it could just slide off at any moment. The house looks like it is trying to hold itself together, like a person trying not to cry.

Bryony walks past it every day without looking through the railings at all, until one day a gust of wind takes her velvet cap and flings it over the top, into the playful branches of a sprawling rhododendron which deposits it at the front door. From the lane she cannot see it, and tears sting her eyelids, large stones tumble in her stomach. She grips the twisted railings and peers through, hoping to see a quick solution. It's just a hat, a little voice tries to tell her, but a bigger voice tells her it isn't. It is a present from father. Had he not asserted how her mother would have liked it, she may not have been so possessive about it.

She rattles the gates in the hope that they will fall open, but they clang, remaining disappointingly steadfast. She has a photograph of her mother in a silver locket round her neck, her bright curls falling round her face. You can just see the brim of a hat in the picture, very much like the one she has just lost. The big voice tells her numerous reasons why she has to make every effort to retrieve it. It isn't just any hat, it is the one that father chose, the one mother would have liked, the last one in the shop, two seasons ago, there simply isn't another one like it. It is unique and irreplaceable.

Now decided, she wonders if there is another way into the grounds. A footpath, guarded by thick nettles runs alongside the wall at the edge of the garden and she can see it might lead to the back of the property. Her woollen knee socks and long coat will afford some protection, and besides, she has to at least try. How hollow and forlorn will she feel if she goes back hatless and has to explain to father that she lost it, but doesn't know how or where and made no attempt to find it? How could she bear his wrath on top of her own stupidity at not being able to wear a hat on a breezy day without it getting lost so easily?

Her feet sink into mulchy leaves and the nettles creep over her socks and scratch at her thighs but they are thinning out now and there is another gate, this time made of wood, crudely hanging in a small arch on the back wall surrounding this melancholy abode. She only has room to take one step backwards in this forgotten alleyway and look up at the rear of this imposing structure. She is closer to the house from this position, so it looks taller. The roof cannot be seen but the windows, she counts six upstairs, are not boarded but resemble gaping black holes, as no light reflects on them as the place backs onto a wooded area.

It's not difficult, the big voice says. You're nearly there.

Just go through the gate, skip round to the front, and pick up the hat. Retrace your steps back here, slip past the nettles, they're all trodden down now anyway, then run back home. No one will be any the wiser. The little voice tries to squeak out, but the big voice has got it all under control.

She is moving her hands up the damp wood, pushing and pushing. She can hear small creaks and sighs as the wood starts to give. It won't take long; she can be in and out in a couple of minutes. She steps back for a moment and plants her gaze on the windows again. There is something about them compelling her to look. She spends a few seconds searching them, inspecting the grey lintels, the matte black panes and the flaking exterior sills. She is braced, expecting to see some kind of movement, and brazenly staring, almost daring one to be made. But there is none, just the age mottled stone mullions and the drain pipe leading from a hole in the wall under one of the windows to draw a riveted line down one side of the house. She suddenly gets a deep feeling of sadness imagining the water seeping out, the life blood trickling away. Then just as she pulls her eyes away, it's there. A pale shape in the window that almost makes her jump. She blinks and looks again but sees nothing but the sad, square window.

Just get the hat, says the big voice. You've come this far. It's only a deserted old place next to the road. It's not like it's in the middle of a wood. She looks behind her seeing the spongy masses of deep green foliage atop the cluster of trees beyond the footpath. The nearest neighbour is only a hundred yards away. Then next door to them a friendly-looking row of terraced houses. Summerscale Lane. She shivers. There is something about the name of the road as well. If it were just Summer Lane it would be fine. Now you really are being ridiculous, says the big voice. Do you want this hat or not? She runs through a scenario where her father looks at her in a very disappointed way, and a tear pricks at her eye again. She does want the hat. She can't imagine a scenario where she gets another that is just as nice and the fat tear rolls down her cheek. She presses the silver locket to her chest, thinks of her mother, and pushes at the wooden gate. It opens stiffly and stops halfway as if there is something behind it. It is just a tight clutch of brambles and weeds. She kicks a few out so that they don't press the gate shut again.

The rear of the house is a testament to decay. There is a door that was once bottle green but most of the paint has flaked off, leaving bare wood that looks somehow naked. There should be a path all the way round the building but each side is filled with foliage. The only way to the front door is through the back door.

There is a small back yard bordered by a high drystone wall which has been colonised by rampant ivy. The stone flags are littered with branches and other debris that has been blown, or thrown in over the years. The house must be nearly two hundred years old. She realises she knows nothing about how people lived then, or what kind of people would have lived here. She knows nothing about this place, except that her hat is here, her beloved hat, probably just thirty feet away from where she is standing now.

There is an old bell push set in the wall near the back door. She has a strong urge to press it, but remembering her unease while looking at the upstairs window, she keeps her hands firmly under control. If there is something in there, the little voice says, but the big voice takes over and says of course there isn't anyone there. If there was, it wouldn't be so neglected would it? Nobody lives like this, do they? She tries the handle while her resolve is dominant, and the door opens smoothly without a murmur, almost as if the house was inviting her in.

A rush of stale air assails her senses, she feels like she has breathed something in. Her throat feels dry, she can taste something like mould, and she has a desperate urge for a glass of water.

It isn't as dark on the ground floor as the lack of light in the upstairs windows would suggest. She stands on the threshold and can see a long, wood-lined corridor leading into the house, at the end of which is a tiled room with an open door. Bathroom? She thinks, and puts one foot into the house.

The little voice is quivering. What if your foot goes through, what if the door shuts behind you, what if someone comes and finds you here, what if the ceiling comes down? The big voice takes over. You can prop the door open with a branch, the ceiling has stayed up this far, it can manage another five minutes while you run through, go out the front and get the hat, and if someone does come you can say you're very sorry, you just wanted your hat and you will be on your way. Besides, there really isn't anyone here, there would be signs of life if there were, there would be sounds, footsteps, voices.

While she still has one foot on the outside of the house, she listens carefully. The only sounds she can hear are the beats of her heart and the faint rustle of the trees behind the house. She is trying not to look anywhere for too long, but she really does want a drink of water. She really does want her hat.

How much better would she feel but for the cool liquid slipping down her throat. She only has to get as far as the tiled room, have a sip, go to the front door, surely that is just round the corner, open the door, get the hat and...come back. It will only take two minutes. She must have been here fifteen already.

When she steps out to get the branch to prop open the door, the feeling of thirst intensifies as if the house has realised it has her now. Ridiculous. How can a house think? It is a pile of stone, slate, and wooden boards. She fixes the branch in the door testing it to make sure it stays open. It is tight. Satisfied, she stands on the step gathering her mettle as if she is going to dive off the highest board into a tiny pool the size of a glass of water. She puts one foot in and tests the boards gingerly. They creak a little but are perfectly stable. She brings her other foot in and is now standing firmly inside.

She takes a deep breath. Two minutes. This will take two minutes. She fixes her eyes

on the tiled room and starts to walk.

Inside the house, everything feels different. It's like a dream: she wants to walk quicker, but she can't. There are icy hands pushing her back as she tries to gain some motion to walk quickly to the tiled room. She feels like she has done two minutes already but she has only done three or four steps with at least twenty yet to do. The soily taste of turf gets stronger and she's gasping for air; it's like she is being buried alive. Her arms ache and she remembers the picture of her mother. She holds it, saying her name over and over. The tiled room is getting nearer.

She pushes open the door, and a sound startles her. A baby! A baby crying, that needy desperate crackling.

She must get the water for the baby as well as for herself. There is a sink with verdigris-stained taps. She twists the one marked cold, it is stuck. A loud clanking as the tired pipes awaken. There isn't a glass. A stream of filthy water starts to dribble out. She turns it harder, the tap shakes then the water starts to run clear. She cups it in her hands and drinks. Someone is behind her. Slowly she turns.

It is her mother, who passed in childbirth, holding her stillborn sister in her arms. She is wearing Bryony's hat.

WET FINGERS

OWEN TOWNEND

Wet
fingers
on
glass
drip
cold
thoughts.

Rain through heavy tears,
dew chilling the night,
snow drowned in puddles,
whetting the Earth's appetite.

Wet fingers
grasp at truth.

Wet fingers
always dry.

JAPAN - 2018

EXTERNAL ADJUDICATOR'S COMPETITION

12 JAPANESE HAIKU

GARETH CLEGG

Once upon a time
In a land far, far away
Samurai Star Wars

In all the rivers
That make up the four islands
Japanese dragons

Dark spirits and ghosts
Flood the ruined Tokyo streets
A bleak future waits

Beautiful brush strokes
Produce art as well as form
To polish sword play

There to teach English
I fell in love with Japan
in all her beauty

Full of poise and charm
The old tea ceremony
I need a cuppa

Miniature flora
Grown to precise and strict rules
Full of care and love

Cherry blossom days
Lead to Cherry blossom nights
Our last Sakura

Red petals on snow
A sign of fury now past
Blades now sheathed in peace

Beloved child of ours
Heart full of joy and beauty
Tears now fill our eyes

Nature's perfect form
Ever present around us
Ruined by humans

The last sight of man
At the end of every day
The eternal night

CHIHIRO

VIVIEN TEASDALE

She didn't realise that the girl had her coils wrapped so tightly around her son until it was too late. But that was a thousand years ago – or so it seemed – and she was still there, in that living graveyard, side by side with the shadows, while her family were long gone. But this story needs to be told, to warn the others.

Kasumi came into their lives when the old woman was coming to the end of her working life and Joji was just beginning to make a success of his. It wasn't surprising that soon there was a wedding and a daughter-in-law, one to be pleased with, even though Chihiro no longer wanted to admit that. Kasumi was attractive, meek, respectful to her elders and a good wife and mother. What more could anyone ask for?

Well, for a start Chihiro asked for sanctuary. Husbands provide for their family, wives raise the children, honour the family ancestors. As a widow she was worth nothing to society except that given by the family status. Sons were expected to support their parents. Now it was Joji's turn to take up the burden, though it was still Chihiro, not Kasumi as was expected, who lit the candles and performed the rituals that honoured those gone from sight, Chihiro who showed the right respect to the lineage. She who ensured that their shades blessed, not cursed them, and Joji followed her lead – for a while.

But still Kasumi showed correct deference to her. 'Honoured Mother of my Husband' the girl used to call her mother-in-law, never her given name. How long was it since that had been heard on anyone's lips or whispered in that soft baritone of Joji's father?

'Honoured Mother of my Husband,' Kasumi said one day, 'soon you will have another generation to love and protect. But the spare room is so small. What can we do?'

Chihiro moved into the tiny space, cordoned off at the back of the house and the firstborn grandson, Akio, took her lovely room that looked out onto the garden. The garden she'd tended for so long, the garden her husband made for her when they first moved to this house on the edge of Tokyo, before Joji was born.

'Honoured Mother of my Husband, we have two lovely boys now. Perhaps we should make the elder sit in the corner, struggling but learning to balance his meals on his tiny lap. The table is so small and there is no room for a larger one.'

From the corner Chihiro could see them eating, laughing together as she looked at their backs and silently begged for a word, but the word was always 'work'. She washed, she cleaned, she cooked, she prayed to their ancestors for help.

'Soba, grandmother,' the boys would say, 'make us cake.' And cake would have to be on the table before Joji came home or they would complain about her lack of respect for the men in the family. Joji would laugh and tell them they weren't quite men yet, but he would glare at his mother and Kasumi would point out that there was very little money for a growing family and cutbacks might have to be made unless everyone did all they could to help in the house. Chihiro worked harder than ever, growing more frail every day.

'Honoured Mother of my Husband, Joji and I plan to go on a journey and want you to come with us. There is a shrine in the north, near Mount Fuji. They say those who make offerings to their ancestors there can obtain great healing. Come with us. We will all offer our prayers that your aches and pains are ended.' Blood had called to blood and she knew her life would change.

The journey was long and arduous, the earth hard, dark and unforgiving. As the land began to rise there was a little more grass, shrubs and then trees, sparsely fighting for existence together. The mountain pointed upwards, its snowy peak facing the sky as if to say 'look at the blueness, at the light, at sunshine. This is where it ends.' It grew darker, colder as the forest began to close in.

'Joji,' Chihiro said, 'we must stop. We must go back while we can still find the way.'

'I know the way, Honoured Mother of my Husband,' Kasumi replied. 'Don't be afraid.' And so they went on, deeper and deeper into the gloom and the silence. Only Chihiro seemed to feel the menace of the place, the buzzing of some otherness around them.

They slept that night close to a black rock, an ice cave deep within it, though they stayed outside, trying to shelter against the slender tree trunks nearby. Joji lit a small fire and warmed saké, which Kasumi served, kneeling before the old woman to pour out the liquid into the cup. Chihiro slept well for the first time in months.

When she awoke, she was alone.

'Joji!' she called and called. She walked around the rock, into the cave entrance, searched all around, inside and out but every path seemed to have disappeared. Tree roots reached out, tripping her up, and small bushes blocked every route she tried. Only thin, starved trees, dripping mist and the shivering whispers of the wind remained as her companions.

Aokigahara. The Sea of Trees. She knew then where she was and why they had brought her there. They say people went there to commit hara-kiri, to take responsibility for their wrongdoing, for their loss of honour. But Chihiro had done nothing wrong then.

She lurched from tree to tree until she finally found some sort of path. In the branches, a small pink strip of fabric showed where someone had been before her. Another, further on, raised her hopes but there were no more. Instead she saw a strong rope, still twisted tightly round spiked vertebrae, the skull slunk down over them and grinning maliciously at Chihiro. 'This is your fate,' it sneered at her, its echoes following as she tried to run, staggering and stumbling, back past the pink markers.

Water was plentiful, but all her knowledge of herbs and medicine was of no use in the dark forest. She walked on, trying to head downhill, trying to mark her way, until the confusion became absolute and she curled up in a hollow in the dark ground and her spirit withdrew, waiting for the rituals to begin. Seven days, forty-nine days, one hundred days with no purification rites performed. The first Obon, the return of the souls to their family home, the calling of shades to the cemetery, to the temple by their family. Chihiro's shade heard nothing, saw no offerings, no lights to welcome it home, saw no dances in its honour. It grew in anger, becoming strong. 'They were right.' Chihiro thought. 'My ancestors have helped me. Here I have no aches, no pains except those in my heart and they feed my ambition.'

She waited. But while she waited, she practised. She watched them walking, slinking, sometimes running into the forest. Sometimes they hovered on the edges, looking this way and that, before turning and walking away. Others marched in, determination on their faces. She left those alone. They were already focussed on their destination.

It was the ones who entered the forest, watching the shadows of the sunset creeping in through the bars of the trees, knowing they could, if they really wanted to, still find their way out. They were the ones who heard an undertone in the noises of the woodland; it whispered of their weaknesses, their dishonour, their only way to atone. Chihiro worked quietly, subtly until in the early hours, when despair is at its zenith, they throw the rope high over the nearest branch and fulfil the purpose that they never really believed, never really intended to accomplish. She watched their ghosts, their yurei, dangling limply beside the body for days, for months. Some drifted away eventually, despairing, defeated. Their shades spread out too thinly among the undergrowth to do more than create an occasional shiver in the leaves. Others rose, stretched and danced, easily gliding out of the forest, back to the ancestral graves, to celebrate the Obon festival that marked the honouring of the ancestors and brought good luck to their descendants.

At her second Obon, Chihiro launched her spirit outwards, grasping other shades who followed the prayers of their families back towards their villages. Unknowing or uncaring, they dragged her with them.

'Now,' she thought, 'I can whisper in Joji's ear that he will never succeed without me. He will try not to listen, think he is just tired. But soon he will begin to doubt his judgement, his ability. He will argue with Kasumi. She will know me and she will fight. I know she will fight.'

And she did. They battled for his mind. She shouted, threatened, tried to dominate. Chihiro hinted, jeered, suggested insidiously until he didn't know which way to turn. She used every trick, all the deception and dishonesty she'd learned in the pits of the forest of death.

He shrank, first in his mind and then in his body. He shrivelled away just as Chihiro had done, inch by inch. He went to the temple, made offerings, vowed to honour his ancestors, his father, his mother, but it was too late. She could not, would not allow herself to hear him.

It wasn't really his fault, but when they finally met again, she could find no mercy. He had abandoned her, left her to rot as they'd supposedly done in ancient times. He didn't recognise her, didn't realise what he'd done, what she'd done, until he felt the first oni's grasp, the yamauba that would devour his flesh, piece by piece for all eternity.

Akio and Nori returned home for their father's funeral, but neither had space in their city flats for his widow. Kasumi was allowed the tiny box room in her former home, which was rented by Joji's cousin. She toiled day after day, until the morning she followed the murmurs in her head and walked out. She was found next day, floating in the river, her head pointing north towards Mount Fuji, her face a screaming mask. Her sons did not return for her funeral, leaving it all to their distant relatives. They were too busy making their living in the distant city of Hiroshima.

Kasumi should have learned to honour the ancestors of Joji's family. But then women had no power in those days and Chihiro didn't realise she would enjoy power so much. The power of neglected kin, of deserted blood. But now she has eternity before her, to walk side by side with vengeance, in all its forms.

JAPANESE TSUNAMI

SUSIE FIELD

Stolen memories
Trapped within decaying walls
Never to be shared.

Waves rising higher
Taking all within their path
Hope lost forever.

Life beneath the sea
Torn and savagely taken
Never forgotten.

Face at the window
Staring into the darkness
Nothing left to see.

Unforgettable
Powerful and intrusive
Showing no mercy.

Howling in the night
Intense and unforgiving
Poised for destruction.

The swell of the sea
A storm on the horizon
All will soon be lost.

It happened so fast
A disappearing landscape
Brutally taken.

Families parted
Searching for missing loved ones
Crying with despair

There's no place to hide
As raging seas lash the coast
Wild and relentless.

OTSUKIMI DREAMS
GARETH CLEGG

The woman stood in a small boat, alone on the lake, head bowed, staring into the depths. Her beautiful white kimono flowed around her at the merest whisper of a breeze. The red paper parasol, shading her pale features from the warm September sun, rippled with the air's passing. All joined the bright blue reflection of the sky mirrored in the glassy stillness of the lake. A scene of idyllic beauty you'd expect to see captured in an artist's mind.

Dread gnawed deep within my gut, and I knew I must save her before something terrible happened. A shiver ran up my spine as I descended into the icy lake. Vivid orange, red and gold rippled across the surface, glorious reflections of autumn's fire near the thickly forested shoreline as I swam to reach her.

The boat looked the same distance ahead, but the shoreline now seemed much further away. The woman maintained her silent vigil, a scene of tranquillity, but I sensed danger. The boat rocked, gently at first, but became violent as the woman fought for balance. I surged across the distance, hand grabbing the edge of the boat to steady it, but in my haste, I tipped it below the water line.

All was silent as she slipped into the watery embrace. The boat sank, drifting like an autumn leaf, escorting her slow descent. A shroud of billowing white surrounded her, small bubbles forming at the edge of her ruby painted lips before escaping back towards the surface.

I thrashed through the water, reaching her in seconds to find unblinking eyes, set into the painted white skin, a sad smile spreading across her face. Cloth whipped out as I reached to free her, tangling my wrists. Wet silk constricted like a vice and, with a sudden yank, sent me plummeting into the depths far below, my lungs burning as darkness approached at a startling rate.

I fought to cry out, but the crushing pressure gripped me. Tiny bubbles formed around my mouth then ran up my face. Like rain on windows, they joined, growing until they escaped back towards their world of air and sky. My blood pumped a steady throbbing rhythm, and white specks danced before me like shooting stars, slowly fading.

My eyes snapped open, vision blurry as if from deep sleep. Bodies swayed, suspended from tangled ropes of kelp, hundreds of them. Hair billowed around them in the submerged cave. I struggled but couldn't move, my mind somehow disconnected from my physical body. In a final show of defiance, I spat out a scream.

Bubbles burst from my last lungful of air, trembling through the water, rising to meet the silvery cave roof. It shimmered like mercury as my final breath touched it, consuming what I was, absorbing and growing.

A red circle drifted on the surface, twisting in an unseen current. The parasol formed a blood-soaked reflection of the huge Otsukimi festival moon. The only evidence that anyone was ever there.

NAMAHAGE

OWEN TOWNEND

Forgive me. It has been years since someone last used my name.

My North Korean captors never gave me this honour. They did not care when they forced me onto their boat at the shore of Niigata.

I had foolishly walked away from a party. A friend of a friend's: I can't even remember who. I was feeling sorry for myself and found staring at the crests of distant waves soothing. As if, when I closed my eyes, the ocean breeze would balance me.

In that very moment two large men grabbed me from behind. One threw a black bag over my head and the other punched me in the stomach.

When they led me to the boat, I found breathing impossible. When it set out, I couldn't tell which was louder: the motor or my heart. One of the men forced me down until we were well away from any witnesses. The cheering of the party faded.

Eventually my captors relaxed and began to amuse themselves. They told me in poor Japanese that I was going to be a prisoner of their Great Leader, that there were many others like me and we would form a carpet for him to walk on.

The humiliation worsened. One of the men reached for my crotch and likened me to 'a comfort woman'. I have been told that I have a soft face for a man.

Eventually the boat stopped and I was dragged onto North Korean land. They did not need to beat me anymore as, by that point, I was too terrified not to comply.

They removed the black bag and I looked into a well-fed, pock-marked face with grey eyebrows arched over tiny black eyes. This was the face of Captain Pak, the high-ranking Korean soldier who would 'keep' me.

He kept me in the basement. When I saw the stained mattress, I wept with joy. It was the only thing in that sparse room but I fell onto it as soon as the door was closed. Though it stank of stale sweat, I hugged it for hours.

I was fed two meals a day, hard bread and a soup with little taste. I soon lost my belly and had to crawl around in the dark with bony arms. I did not have a mirror or a razor and so could not trim my beard or hair. I must have looked a wild man.

It wasn't too long before I saw my first visitors: Captain Pak again with two children in tow. They stared at me from behind his khaki trousers. I could not understand the Korean he barked but it seemed like Pak was teaching them a lesson, one which they promised again and again they had learnt before he finally let them leave.

These visits happened regularly over the course of a year. I even began to mark time by it. As awful as it felt to be the subject of fear in little children, it remained a break of light in the general darkness.

I knew what I was to Captain Pak now. I was his

Namahage, a demon that scares children into good behaviour. I do not know what the North Korean equivalent would be.

Eventually these visits stopped: the children must have been well on their way to becoming honourable adults. Perhaps they were part of the effort to abduct more of my people under some misplaced belief that this was retribution for what the Imperial Japanese Army once did to their country.

For the longest time there were no visits whatsoever. Some days I screamed; others I fell silent. I began to wonder what more of a service I could provide Captain Pak. If nothing, then I was surely dead. Nevertheless, he did finally visit me again, dragging a stool.

I had never seen Captain Pak so distressed. He sat and spoke at length, at first with curt resolution, then with ear-splitting anger and at last with desperate sadness.

At first it was a small chipping away of his resilience but then, with every subsequent visit, it became clearer and clearer that the man was coming apart. Whenever he mentioned Kim Jong-Il by name, he let go a single tear.

As with the Namahage visits, Captain Pak's confessions stopped suddenly and completely. For months I lay in darkness, mind racing at all I had heard. Pak had shamed himself, bared his soul to a demon. Not even that. A wretched foreigner. I would be disposed of soon enough.

Then the soldiers came again. They carried my atrophied body out of the basement and sat me in front of men in suits.

I knew they were Japanese as soon as I saw them but tried not to make a fool of myself. North Koreans were still outside the door, after all, and they would surely savour the chance to meeting.

The lawyers, my countrymen, told me that they were negotiating my release, that they were having some difficulty securing me.

In the meantime I was to stay close by in special accommodation. It had a bed that did not slide beneath me and three square meals offered. I cried for hours.

When I was done, I showered, cut my hair and trimmed my beard. The face underneath no longer felt soft. And yet all it took was a pair of scissors to chase the Namahage away.

The lawyers came to collect me only a couple of days later. I slept for most of the flight back to Tokyo, fitfully but safe.

Now I am home again and 2004, this year of my liberation, has almost passed. The other abductees are required to return to North Korea as part of the agreement, though I doubt Japan will let us return to such squalor.

As for me, I hope never to see Captain Pak again or that basement room where I became a grotesquerie.

I am no man's demon.

THE DEATH SEEKER

GEMMA ALLEN

What am I doing here? I am leaving behind the breathing world. Is it the right thing to do?

The entry into the forest is foreboding. Thick, dark, telling you there is no entry.

I progress along the path. A rope dangles in front of me. Looking up, I see the remains of a figure, newly departed. A life lost, relatives grieving. But I don't pause to consider the after effects. If I did, I would never proceed.

More bones cross my path, and then a pair of shoes. I can't see the bones that go with the footwear. They are lined up precisely, side-by-side and with the laces inside. They look unworn, maybe bought specifically for this last trip. If I were leaving the forest I might welcome a brand-new pair of shoes. But for now they remain. Eventually they will fall apart and be welcomed into the forest, which will take what it wants from the unnatural materials.

Leaves crunch underfoot, their colours alternating between bright red and rich orange. A layer of frost sits on top, dimming the vividness of the colours, and so the leaves vary from the brightest to palest of shades.

In amongst the leaves, a group of bones sits collected atop a rock. Someone on their own journey has spent time arranging these human remnants carefully. Why? It won't change anything.

I reach out and pick up one bone, not yet ravaged by nature. A recent death, then. Would someone rearrange my bones? Or would that be disturbing my death, or my spirit as it departs? But it might bring that still-breathing human some comfort; it would only be another death-seeker that came this far in. I can't think of another reason to do it. Maybe it would be worth doing.

I continue along the well-trodden path, past more collections of bones, these ones left alone. This is how everyone ends up here. No one gets out. This is my fate.

I must be nearly there. The tree trunks are growing thicker, the ground steeper. After the peaceful path that I began on, this is claustrophobic. As though the forest was leaning in, watching me, drawing me in. The tree roots are all tightly packed now, and I take care not to stumble. Not all the trees are appropriate. I'm looking for a sturdy branch, one I can reach to loop the rope over, but not too close to the ground.

The branches keep blocking my way. If you want to reach your destination you have to fight, the forest is telling me. I pull at jagged branches, cutting my hands and catching clothes on the sharp ends. The fight wakens my anger, and I push myself on to reach the end.

Finally, I reach my destination. A huge tree, so tall I can't see the top.

I lay my rucksack on the ground and draw out my rope. The noose is already prepared, and double checking it confirms the tightness. Kneeling on the ground, I hear a bird chirp, interrupting the oppressive silence. The creature has a life to lead, possibilities to explore. A pang takes my breath away momentarily.

The branch presents itself to me, bowing slightly as if it is asking to be used. I attempt to grab it, but the branch snaps upwards, out of my hands. Throwing the rope over it also results in failure. The forest will not allow me to do this easily.

A crunch fills me with dread. Is there someone else around? I can't help but feel annoyed; how dare they interrupt my moment. There are so many other minutes, hours, days for someone to choose, why now?

I peer into the forest's deliberate dimness, trying to see this other person intruding on my space. But I can't see anything, apart from the odd shiver from the branches around me. No more sounds are forthcoming, so maybe I imagined it.

This place is spooky enough to cause you to imagine all sorts. People inevitably say the forest is haunted. With all the dead bodies decaying within it, there are bound to be such reports. I had never believed the rumours, of course. It would be nice to think that I would meet the spirit of my mother, still present here after twenty-odd years, but I know that won't happen. Even if it is possible, there is no point. What would she tell me about her life and death that I don't already know? I also don't want her to know I am copying her path, choosing the same fate despite the impact her death had on me.

A bird chirped cheerfully – the same one? This is it; the time has arrived. I check around to make sure there are no other people, no nearby bones and that my rope is ready. After another attempt to hook the rope over the branch, I am finally ready.

Or am I? Doubts, which I thought I had banished, begin

to circulate round my mind. I find my resolve. This is a one-way trip, always has been. I am not going back. This may be suicide, but back out there is a living hell.

The forest appears to whisper to me. There are no fully formed words, but a reassuring soft hum. The sound gradually becomes louder and begins to pulse. The pulsing gets faster and I feel a sense of urgency. I must do this and I must do it now. I slip the noose over my head and pause. This is the last chance to change my mind.

And then the tree trunk I am standing on seems to disappear, and the branch I am using stretches higher into the sky.

The noose grabs me

TOKYO PRIME

GARETH CLEGG

Staring at the sky
Life a fleeting memory
Rain now fills my eyes

New Tokyo: 2067 - Shinjuku District - 03:17

The black skies wept angry tears through the glowing city dome, hammering on the cruiser's roof like the heavy thrashing beat of Tek-metal—it was all the rage with the kids.

A couple dashed across the street, dancing between puddles of vibrant neon. The girl's pink spray-on latex and thigh-length boots reflected from the glass storefronts, almost as garish as the signs above her. Just another working-girl, hooker, streetwalker—I'm not even sure what the correct term is anymore. I don't judge—twenty-odd years on the force does that to you. She, and the hundreds like her—male, female, exotics—weren't the problem; it was the pimps and the gangs that ran them who needed taking down. Anyhow, I was on a break.

A low growl issued from my stomach. When did I last eat? Six, maybe eight hours ago? I checked my skinwatch— it was oh-three-seventeen—damn, how long did it take to pick up fast-food?

Rain roared as the passenger door flew upward. Shin pushed two cartons along the central console and slammed the bulletproof titanium closed behind him. Water beaded on the scarlet plastifoam packaging from the Red Tiger Noodle House. Tiny streams dripped onto the leather seating as steam escaped the neatly folded packages. The aroma reminded me of long stakeouts and hours of boredom.

"Chopsticks or fork?" he asked.

"You're joking, right?"

Shin laughed, water bouncing from his black wedge of hair. It somehow maintained its perfect shape against all the laws of physics I knew—then again, it had a similar consistency to plastifoam. Three months ago, this kid was patrolling the streets. Now he was a junior detective, and my newest partner.

"Yeah, yeah. Everyone knows gaijin can't use chopsticks."

"Fuck you," I said, grabbing a set of plasti-wrapped sticks. "I've lived in New Tokyo longer than you've been out of short pants." It was a running joke in the department. As the only Westerner, they called me gaijin—foreigner. They thought it was funny—I thought they were dicks.

Shin was an okay kid, but he must have done something awful in a past life to be stuck with me as a partner. I'd made more than my fair share of enemies—disgruntled city officials, gangs, and even high-profile members of the Yakuza. The legendary crime gang now had seats on the Council, but they still had their fingers in lots of unsavoury shit. I didn't buy into their modern, respectable front as many others did. That had led to serious shitstorms with my inspector.

Screw him, I thought. Screw them all. I joined the force in New York twenty-four years ago - or was it twenty-five now? Either way, I'd done well and prided myself on keeping clean all that time. It was my own personal code of Bushido if you like.

"Hey, Drake. Is it true what they say back at the office?"

"What do they say?" I asked, taking a slurp of noodles.

"That you shot another officer?"

"Yeah, but it's not as exciting as they make out in the locker room."

"And you got busted for it? Demoted to sergeant?"

"Look, kid," I said. The chopsticks paused halfway towards my mouth, thick red globs of spicy sauce threatening to stain my shirt. "Don't believe everything you hear. Plenty of assholes work in this department, and grudges grow over the years. It's best to keep out of office politics and get on with the job. Do your shift, go home and enjoy your downtime. Anyhow, who wants to be an inspector with all that fucking paperwork?"

The radio burst into life. "All units, we have an 11-97: Officer in need of assistance. Anyone in the vicinity, proceed to the apartment building at the end of Hokuban Drive. Patrol unit twenty-three responded to a report of gunshots fired. His emergency transponder has activated."

I gunned the engine. "That's less than ten minutes from here."

As Shin replied to dispatch, we skidded onto the main street with lights and sirens blazing through the early morning traffic.

"Shit," Shin said. "His bio-monitor flatlined."

I punched the override and took manual control. Radio signals raced through the ether, clearing a path through the traffic system.

Hokuban Drive was in one of the older districts of the city, dirty and run-down. Bright flashes of blue and red reflected from the puddles, casting shifting shadows along the front of the ageing apartment building. The steady drumming on the car's roof became thunderous as the doors slid upwards. I caught Shin's arm before exiting. "No heroics, kid. I'll take the lead. You back me up." Shin didn't complain.

Water splashed into my shoe as I stepped into the rain. Well, that's great—a whole damn street and I find the only pothole.

Shin drew his pistol and scanned the area while I headed to the other police vehicle, the sole source of illumination. It was empty but still locked. I pulled my E-CaRD, and it chirped to life, the transparent screen brightening as it recognised my biometrics. Four icons popped into view—me, Shin and the two vehicles. I tapped the other vehicle's icon and started the emergency override.

A soft blip from the E-CaRD echoed from the vehicle as its maglocks disengaged with a heavy thud. The door opened, and I slid into the driver's seat out of the downpour and sealed myself inside.

The diagnostics matched the dispatcher's description of events—nothing out of the ordinary. No signs of tampering

—that was enough for me. "Everything checks out here, Shin. Meet me at the entrance."

"Drake, I've lost radio contact with Central. It's static on every band."

"Okay, we'll deal with that later. Let's get inside."

The building stood in darkness. Orange light flickered before my left eye as the Head-Up-Display started. I switched to Infrared, and my brain baulked for a second as everything shifted to grey. It was a typical reaction as the video feed from the cam punched the visuals onto my retina.

Other than a few mailboxes and a single stairwell leading upward, the stark lobby was empty. With no trace of disturbance, I took the stairs, reached the first turn and stopped. Corners and doorways were where the shit went down. I slowed to a cautious pace, weapon held out before me.

I'd done it a thousand times, but my stomach still fluttered as I pushed the E-CaRD round the corner. The feed to my HUD showed everything was clear. I inched around, then motioned Shin to join me as I continued to the landing.

Something bright flashed in the IR view. I stopped, kneeling at the top of the stairs where a ceiling light flickered at the end of the hall. So, the power wasn't completely dead then.

Most of the doors lining the corridor hung open, broken furniture and household items spilt into the passage. I pointed for Shin to watch the hallway while I checked the corner, scanning the next flight of stairs. Empty again.

"We'll check this level before we go any further," I

whispered. Shin nodded, following as I stalked towards the first door on the left. It hung open into the hall—that was unusual—most apartments opened inwards. Deadbolts lay twisted on the ground, sheared off, and that took a vast amount of force. The apartment looked as if someone had shaken it like a snow globe. I'd only seen devastation of this magnitude once before, during the great earthquake in forty-five which led to rebuilding Tokyo. That had collapsed half the city, ripping it apart as core structures failed under the massive earth surges. Whatever happened here had caused no structural damage.

It was quiet within, and I squeezed through between the shattered frames of broken furniture littering the place. My HUD struggled to identify the twisted shapes and settled for creating outlines.

The E-CaRD vibrated as a red outline grew around a puddle on the transparent display. Temperature readings flashed up, showing the slowly congealing pool of blood. I found the body under a stainless steel work-surface, but the guy was beyond the help of a med-team.

Shin's voice filtered through from the doorway, low but insistent. "Drake?"

With no sign of anyone else in the apartment, I picked my way back to the door. "What's up, kid?"

"I heard something upstairs."

"You sure? Not just getting jittery in the dark?"

Shin pointed upwards. "Jittery, sure. But there was definitely noise from up there."

"Shit."

I hated leaving areas unchecked, but this would take forever. "Single body in there, male Japanese adult, crushed by all the crap in his room being flung around."

"Flung around how?"

"If I didn't know better, I'd have said earthquake, but no damage to the building, so—"

A dull thud from above stopped me in my tracks.

"Okay, kid. Change of plan. Follow me and remember that corners and doorways are our worst enemies. Stay sharp and keep checking our six."

We reached the stairwell, the feeling in my stomach gnawing. Shin controlled the angles well and remembered to check behind too. He must have been sick of my constant mantra of corners and doorways. Still, as long as he followed my advice, he wouldn't end up paralysed like my last partner.

The smell hit us before we saw anything. The coppery tang in the air, sickly sweet, was quickly drowned by the foetid stench of shit. Blood drenched the top half of the stairs ahead, viscous, dripping like wax from ageing candles. There was a lot—more than one body's worth.

The sheer volume of blood made it a tough first murder gig for the kid. He retched, but he was doing better than most rookies.

"Hey, Shin." He stared up at me, face pale, beads of sweat forming on his brow. "I know it looks awful, but you got this. Just remember your scene of crime training. You'll be fine."

"But why does it smell so bad?"

I grimaced. "Yeah, that happens a lot with stiffs. The muscles lose their ability to clench and keep the shit on the inside. Not pleasant, but you get used to it."

He muttered 'Fuck' under his breath—I didn't let on I'd

heard. "You ready for this?" I asked. "You can take a breather if you need it."

"No, I've come this far. I'm in for the long run."

"That's the spirit." I clapped him on the shoulder and climbed the last few steps, keeping tight to the wall. It had two effects, giving a better view of the landing above and staying out of most of the filth. I'd walk through blood and shit if I needed to, but these were new shoes.

The hallway was a gore-splattered nightmare. Talk about a baptism of fire. If the kid made it through this, he'd be a damned veteran. Either that or pensioned off with mental trauma—we used to call it PTSD, but that's a non-PC term nowadays - fucking bureaucrats.

Ruined bodies sprawled among the destruction. Blood smeared everywhere—across the floor, up the walls and even on the ceiling. I didn't blame Shin when he gave an apologetic gesture and coughed up the remains of his noodles in the corner.

When he'd done, tears streaked his pale face. It wasn't surprising. That sauce had been spicy on the way down—heaven knew how it felt as remnants dribbled from his nose. To his credit, he pulled himself together, wiping the greasy stains away on his sleeve. The steaming pile of stringy red vomit matched the surrounding gore, but I didn't mention it. Poor bastard had enough to deal with right now.

A creak of something along the hall snapped me back into focus. I motioned for Shin to stay where he was, but he shook his head, drawing his pistol and waving me forward.

Resilient son of a bitch.

As we waded through the wreckage, my E-CaRD chirped again. The image of a handgun dissolved into a wire-frame revealing the internal mechanism. Red outlines showed two rounds were missing—they didn't even let us sniff the barrel anymore.

"What's it found?" Shin asked.

"Jesus, kid. Don't rely on the tech."

"Well, it spotted it before you did. The clue's in the name —Evidence Capture and Retrieval Device—they're cool. Why not use them?"

"Yeah, it's good at finding stuff, but it takes away the art of detection. Don't let it become a crutch. Remember, you might not have it to hand when you need to make a snap decision."

Shin shrugged. "Whatever."

Many of the newer kids depended on the damn things to do all the heavy lifting, and it showed to old-timers like me. Their reliance on the tech led to skimping on the actual detective work, and they just followed procedure from the device. All the essential skills, honed over years on the streets, replaced by iCop.

The rounds fired meant this could be the source of the disturbance the other officer came to investigate, but so far, no signs of the uniform.

Something scraped in the next room along, and I pushed tight against the outside wall, beckoning Shin to join me. I signalled for him to cover the entrance.

I'd learnt to trust this old cop's gut. It had saved me more than once. So let them laugh back at the station - but I was still here years after many younger colleagues were feeding the recyclers.

I showed Shin three fingers, two, one.

The view of the room opened as I burst through, and Shin popped around the doorframe at waist level while I scanned for danger. Piles of broken furniture created bizarre sculptures where they'd fallen. A slight flash of red rushed across my HUD, and the heavy thump of Shin's weapon sent splinters exploding as furniture disintegrated from the shot.

A scream tore through the darkness, and I forced Shin's arm, and his pistol, towards the floor. "Hold your fire!"

His face was white. "What the fuck?"

"You heard the scream, right?"

He was panting, eyes fixed on me.

"Okay?" I asked. He nodded, his breathing heavy, and I released my grasp. It still amazed me how all those years of Aikido came flooding back, my body moving instinctively. That's muscle memory for you—another reason experience is king.

"Hey," I called out to the dark room. "NTPD, we're here to help."

TSUNAMI

SARA BURGESS

The Tsunami which engulfed Japan on March 11, 2011, is recorded as starting at 2:46 p.m. local time. This is the exact time when the great sea monster with glass eyes and scales made of jade awakes from a deep slumber. As his great shuttered lids start to push upwards displacing thousands of tons of shimmering silt on the sea bed, the people of Sendai at first feel only a slight shudder, barely enough to shake the tassels on a lampshade.

The creature is Okasa, the only son of Jishin Namazu, the bringer of deathly water. He flexes his muscles, feeling the wall of rock jab into his spine which stretches for some three hundred miles in a geological fault off the north east coast of Japan. The gargantuan plates grind as he wriggles his tail and thrusts the first battery of shockwaves which hurtle along beneath the ocean, heading towards the north east coastline. He opens his vast mouth to take in a gulp of seawater to swill his fetid insides, unleashing another immense power surge which travels through the water at the speed of a jet plane towards the Sendai coast. When it hits the mile high ridge beneath the surface the water rears up, a great wall of welling ocean ready to strike.

Takeo is ready for the coming disaster, for he and Okasa are old friends. Outwardly, Takeo Tanaka is a smart business man who has been making wise investments, until recently. His slick, silk, raven-black hair glistening with a cobalt-blue hue and his chiselled jawline gives him the appearance of a manga hero. Inwardly, Takeo is no ordinary man, and steeped in tales of a mythical past, he is Daidarabotchi, a powerful giant responsible for forming this exquisite archipelago in the volcanic straits of the North Pacific Ocean.

He who lovingly formed the sweet and ethereal islands of Japan will not take Okasa's threat lying down. He considers everything contained in this place, the most beautiful country on earth, sacred. The jagged mountain ranges like razor sharp teeth, the opulent glades dripping with cascades of purple wisteria and crimson spider lily, the sapphire and emerald lakes glittering like jewels in a prince's crown, even the gleaming skyscrapers in the cities scratching the underbelly of the heavens make his heart swell with pride.

Niko has no idea that her husband has discovered such a pedigree, nor that their son must therefore be part man, part giant. As the great tower of water heads full tilt for the eastern seaboard of Japan, its curved waves splashed with white foam only pausing for a second before striking the inauspicious flatlands north of the Abakuma River. Mother and son are thankfully at home on the fiftieth floor of the Midtown Building, Tokyo, in their suite in the Ritz-Carlton Hotel. She is blissfully unaware of the battle in which her husband is about to engage, a far cry from the deal wrangling boardrooms of his demanding regular day job, while the boy Teru happily plays with a large toy truck with real headlights. As she listens to his blissful babbling, she becomes aware of a change in the air pressure. Her ears pop. The atmosphere seems to be holding its breath, as if trying to pretend it isn't there. Nevertheless, she attributes this to living so high up, and thinks nothing of it until she happens to look out of the window.

Takeo has seen enough from the vantage point in his office. He must confront Okasa. His pretty personal assistant, Aimi, tries to get through to him. Her concern is increasing following the deal-breaker collapse with Vladimir, the latest Russian oligarch on Takeo's list. He has not been himself for some time.

'Tanaka San,' she says, only the slightest hint of desperation showing in her voice. 'The tsunami is upon us. We must find high ground.'

Takeo turns to stare at her, his dark brown eyes almost black, his straight eye brows dipping in the middle like a bridge breaking in a storm. His voice, when it comes, is much deeper than usual. He fires the words as if spitting out balls of lead:

'Ushi no toki mairi.' The walls of the office shake as if they were made of paper. The light fitting above their heads quivers, but it is not this which makes the girl go pale. He says it again; the ancient curse to summon a yokai:

'Ushi no toki mairi.' The old stories say that uttering the summons three times will bring the fearsome yokai to the aid of the speaker. In modern Japan, the stories are a far cry from the days of yore, but the way he says it frightens her. And she can't really be sure whether it is the tsunami shaking the walls or the force of some long undead creature coming to her employer's aid.

She shakes herself free of the ridiculous notion. They

have to get out of here. She can see the sky blackening through the window and hear the shouts of frightened people. There is the far off sound of rushing water.

'Tanaka San!' she cries out, now desperate for him to follow her, hoping the uncharacteristic volume in her voice will make him snap out of whatever psychosis is gripping him. She knows that fear can make people behave in strange ways. She offers her hand and starts for the door, but he brushes it aside and runs for it, bursting the door open with a guttural kiai. She can hear his rapid descent as he clatters down the corridor into the quickly rising water. She follows him with some relief that at least he is leaving the building, but also a tinge of fear. As he exploded through the doorway, she was convinced there were sparks coming out of his eyes.

Niko is peering through the window trying to focus on the fuzzy white line on the horizon. It is normally a broad stroke of blue somewhere above the clusters of geometric concrete, sprouting up seven hundred feet below like digital mushrooms. Something doesn't feel right. The quiet humming of Teru as he makes engine noises while moving his truck on the back of the sofa seems to fade as it slowly dawns on her what the thickening white line means. Tsunami.

With that realisation, she has a sudden sinking sensation, like an elevator dropping to the next floor too quickly. She has an overwhelming urge to scoop up Teru and run till she realises, that on the fiftieth floor, she is probably in the best place to survive a tsunami. Now she has the word in her mind, she can feel the building swaying. A nauseous feeling overtakes her and she has to sit down. Teru spots her and toddles over to cling to her knee, a crumpled expression upon his sweet face. She wonders what other people are doing and another realisation hits her like a train. The walls in one of the most expensive places to live in the world are built to ensure privacy, so silence is to be expected. But a cursory examination of the immediate corridors and a few doorbells later she finds that she and Teru appear to be the only people up there.

And with that understanding comes the third thing to bowl her over; her husband is in the office today, next to the coast. The elevator in her stomach drops another three floors and she moans, gripping Teru to her chest making him whimper. She picks him up and goes over to the window, an activity he normally finds calming as he coos over the astonishing view. But he must sense his mother's anxiety as she gazes at the sinister white line wavering under the stained skies, its very existence unnerving. For a second she imagines how it must feel to be there. She is deafened by the screams and the roar of the water and so shuts it out again feeling helpless. She must speak to him. There must be a helpline. When she flicks on the television, her worst fears are confirmed.

The screen shows cars being swept down the white water rapids that were once streets. The sound is the old World War Two warning siren, for anyone not yet convinced this is an emergency. There is a map of Japan superimposed on the film with a thick red line down the Sendai coastline, like a gash indicating where the main danger zone is located. Then the picture changes to show people running wild, people being knocked over by rushes of water, a voiceover telling people to stay away, a number to ring for news of loved ones. Thankfully, she snatches up her cell phone and presses the numbers. Engaged. Now she has the number she can keep fetching it from the phone's memory every eight seconds till someone picks up.

When Aimi gets out of the building, Takeo is nowhere to be seen. All she can do is follow the people sloshing through the churning water heading for the nearest tall building several blocks away. People from all walks of life are sailing past in one way or another: men wading up to their chests with several small children on their shoulders, makeshift buoyancy aids holding up women with sad faces, and the street, taxis and cars floating by with people on the roofs. Aimi desperately scours the faces to see if any is Takeo, but none is. He has gone, taken his chances, followed his demon.

After twenty three attempts someone does pick up. Niko is so thankful she can hardly remember what she is supposed to be saying. She is aware she is babbling, blathering, getting words mixed up, and the person on the end of the line is trying to inject some order into the proceedings. Neither is making a connection with the other. Eventually she manages to shout her husband's name into the phone.

'Takeo Tanaka,' she shouts, 'Takeo Tanaka,' as if the person didn't hear. Then she is overcome with a tearful gulping sob as the person says they have not heard that name. She throws the phone onto the floor and stands rocking Teru in her arms.

Takeo has Okasa's dappled face firmly in mind as he pushes the other way against the people, against the water, against reason, heading for the coast. He feels the strength of ten men as he goes to meet his nemesis. After all these centuries their day has come. He will confront the monster in his true guise. He will punish the wretch for daring to rise up against his beloved country, now plunged into a seething, broiling soup of dun-coloured water.

'Ushi no toki mairi,' he shouts into the watery air and

feels the yokai he has summoned carry him along, pushing off any who try to make him turn round and go to safety. 'Ushi no toki mairi,' he jibbers. To all who observe him he is a mad man, but in his mind he is a prophet, at one with the ethereal beings at his side in their grey shrouds and imbued with the strength of ten oxen. They carry him along, one at each shoulder, till they get to the roaring mouth of the beast still rolling in with breaker after breaker smashing his country to pieces. In his mind's eye he sees the maw of his foe, laughing at him, taunting him, beneath the waves. With a final cry, he drives into it, feeling his spiritual companions pulling him down, down, further down than he ever thought was possible.

After what seems like hours, with the spectacular sunset lighting up the apartment, Niko awakes from where she had fallen asleep on the floor. Teru is playing with his truck watching its headlights throw beams into the gloom. For a moment she has forgotten her despair of before, cocooned as she is in the luxurious building seven hundred feet above the bustling Tokyo streets. She feels a chill as her doorbell chimes. She wraps a shawl around herself and goes to see who it can be. Then, as her memories return, she almost runs to the door, hoping for news of her husband.

Yes! Through the spyhole she can see three figures, one has the same glorious hair, that ebony black tinged with blue. She feels a surge of warmth as she fumbles to open the door, but when she does her mouth falls open and her face freezes in horror. The two figures in grey melt into nothing, leaving the watery wraith of her husband, his hair matted and festooned with sea debris, and his body wearing nothing but a shroud. She sinks to her knees, for now she has her answer.

TYRANT

NICK STEAD

It was a night touched by destiny. A night touched by the most powerful of kami, manifesting in the great storm raging overhead and battering the land with nature's fury. A night touched by the gods themselves.

Lightning rent the sky, cracks in the heavens through which rain pelted. Wind howled louder than even the greatest of wolf packs, the elements combining to assault the earth. Such was its force, trees bowed before it and even the walls of the great temples shook. And above the roar of the mighty Ryujin, a woman's screams of agony rang out.

The woman screamed again as she fought to bring her baby into the world. Her husband had seen to it that she was surrounded by only the greatest and most experienced of attendants – not just women specialising in childbirth and physicians knowledgeable in all the innermost workings of the flesh, but also the wisest of clerics and miko attuned to all the spiritual dangers present during labour. These holy men and women were entrusted with the vital task of warding off hungry ghosts. One little mistake and the ghosts would prey on mother and newborn in their moment of weakness, a moment when the boundary between the living and the dead blurred so that new life might easily become new death. But that must not happen this time, for this was not just any birth.

Her screams were coming faster now. Their baby's arrival was surely not far off, and Emperor Kaito added his own prayers to those of the priests, calling on the kami of his ancestors to add their protection and lend their strength to the empress. But mostly he prayed to the dragon kami and the great Ryujin himself, even as the god of sea and storms continued to voice his displeasure in the torrent lashing against the palace walls.

No sooner had the emperor finished his prayer than another bolt of lightning struck directly overhead, splitting the sky asunder with a flash bright enough to turn night to day. Then the darkness rushed back in, and his wife's screams came to an abrupt end.

Kaito felt certain his prayers had been answered. Surely even the gods recognised the importance of this child, for this was the future of Japan. And of all the gods, who should come to their aid but the dragon deity? He whose blood still ran strong in the imperial dynasty. But something was wrong.

Silence had fallen within the palace. No baby's cries replaced those of the empress, no female attendants cooing over the newborn and offering their congratulations. No, there was only the storm declaring the power of the elements.

Kaito strode towards the specially prepared chamber, reaching for the sliding door with shaking hands. He entered to the sweet smell of incense and the glow of hundreds of candles, yet for all their rituals and their prayers, the clerics had failed to keep the evil spirits at bay.

The shame in their eyes was plain to see, even as they hastened to bow before him.

His gaze fixed on the cushions where his exhausted wife lay, and the crimson puddle of impurity at her feet. Then it slid to Sakura, settling on the tiny body in her arms, covered in that same impurity.

Sakura had also bowed to her ruler but she straightened then and gave him a sad shake of her head. He still held out his arms to receive the newborn and only once he cradled the corpse of his son would he accept his heir had been born dead, leaving them with this empty shell – broken promises of what might have been.

Worse still, it seemed the dragon had granted his blessing, evidenced by the serpentine mark round the baby's right eye. If the boy had lived, he would undoubtedly have grown to be one of the greatest emperors in the history of Japan. But such was the fickle nature of the ocean god – he had gifted the child with such potential, yet he had not seen fit to defend him from the attack of scavenging ghosts. It was beyond cruel.

"Everybody out!" Kaito ordered.

He could see the uncertain glances that passed between his subjects but they did as he bid them, leaving him alone with his wife and stillborn son. The empress seemed to be too drained to realise what was going on but he knew what he had to do then. There was only one kami left to pray to, and so he called on Izanami, she who was the first woman and the first to die. She alone had the power to help them now.

This time his prayers went unanswered. Defeated, he looked back down at the son who had been stolen from him by the wretches doomed to wander the earth as ravenous spirits, ever hungering for whatever scraps of food they might find but never satiated. No doubt they would continue to feed on the baby's flesh until there was nothing left, as if he had never been conceived.

Kaito knelt and placed the tiny corpse on a cushion, resigned to saying his last goodbyes when there came the unmistakable tickle of something crawling across his cheek. He brushed the creature away, but seconds later another appeared on his hand, and yet more could be felt on the inside of his clothes and the skin beneath. He leapt up and sought to rid himself of the repulsive invaders, only to find more insects and other unwholesome things at his feet, swarming across the floor in a sea of stick thin limbs and bloated brown and black bodies. But the true horror stood behind him.

"Why do you summon me back to the land of the living?" came her voice, beautiful and melodious as any songbird.

He turned to face her, the flames on each of the candles dying as he did so, plunging the room into darkness. His mortal eyes struggled to pick her out in the shadows, the goddess visible as no more than a vague human shape in the gloom.

"My son," he managed, his voice faltering as he succumbed to fear once more. "Has his soul gone to Yomi?"

Izanami did not answer, but the room was suddenly filled with the sounds of a baby's cries, as it should have been from the moment of birth. And though he could not see through the darkness, he felt certain she was cradling his son's spirit.

"Then, if he is now in your care, I would ask you to find it in your heart to return him to us, and give him a chance at life."

"And why would I do that?" she asked, sounding amused.

"Please," he begged. "Yomi is no place for a child. There is no joy or laughter in that land, nor any of the beauty of this one. He is of imperial blood, and he deserves to experience all the wonders of life before being claimed by death."

"Thousands enter Yomi every day, many of them children. Why should your son be granted a second chance at life? Does his lineage truly make him more deserving than any of them?"

"Ryujin has marked him for greatness. I believe he will do much for our people, if he lives."

His eyes were beginning to adjust. He watched the figure tilt her head, as though considering him. "He has not yet eaten from our hearth and so it is possible. But I ask again, why should I allow him a second chance at life? What will you give me in return?"

"What do you ask of me?"

There was a pause, then she straightened her head, the shadow strong and tall now. "For the soul of your son, I require another to take his place. You may name anyone in the palace but you must do so immediately. Remember, we are not really here. As I once told my husband, I am one with the land of the dead now, and I can never leave. The same will be true for your boy if he eats at our hearth."

"Anyone in my palace?"

"Yes. Choose wisely."

Kaito could feel the weight of his decision pressing down on him. Of course he had his enemies; what ruler didn't? But he knew of none currently within the palace walls. He was about to condemn someone to death, someone guilty of no crimes, who had done nothing but serve. How could he make such a terrible decision?

The empress began to stir, her voice weak. "Where is my baby?"

Kaito looked at her, and his choice became clear.

"I name my wife, Asami," he said.

"Your wife?" Izanami asked.

"Yes. She is clearly ill, and perhaps bound for Yomi anyway," he answered, thinking to himself that he also had no further need of her now she had provided him with a son. He had his concubines, whom he loved more than he had ever loved her. "Take her now, and spare her the suffering she might otherwise endure in the grip of her sickness."

"Then I accept."

The emperor's eyes widened at the realisation there were shapes moving around them. Another chill ran through him when he saw they were prowling towards Asami.

Flames burst back into life on the end of each candle, casting light on a scene which should have had no place outside of nightmares. For those shapes were revealed as none other than the hungry ghosts, made visible to mortal eyes in Izanami's presence.

Hideous faces fixated on his wife, a distortion of the human features they'd once had, twisted and made bestial by their own bad karma. Mouths gaped like the jaws of ravening dogs, their tongues snaking out towards their prey. Yet despite their otherwise wasted forms, their bellies bulged with all the food they'd scavenged from the earthly plane, so much so that those bloated stomachs brushed the floor. And yet still they hungered for more.

Worse still was the sight of Izanami striding towards her

prize. Kaito's gaze roamed over the withered body, her frame as bony as those of the ghosts. His stomach turned nauseous at the sight of greying skin turning to fleshy slush, sloughing from her skeleton to reveal patches of the rotting muscles beneath. There was no doubting the truth of what she'd told him. The goddess was truly one with Yomi now.

Izanami turned to glance at him, through eyes surrounded by sunken tissue, her sockets clearly visible. No trace of beauty remained. There was no cartilage where her nose had been and her jawbones were bare on one side, giving her a macabre grin. Only thin strands of hair remained on her head but perhaps worst of all was the sight of more of those unwholesome creatures now covering the floor wriggling across her body. Maggots and other insects of the grave fell from her limbs with every step.

"I will take Asami," she said, voice no longer that of a songbird. It was now the croak of a dying woman, the last breath sighing through a body becoming a corpse. "But I warn you, in sacrificing your own wife you will doom all of Japan. Your son's soul will fester in the evil of your choice made this night, and his rule will bring only misery and death."

Too late, the emperor realised he had angered her by offering Asami, just as her husband had angered her by leaving her in Yomi when he had seen the truth of her decaying form. But it was this deal or nothing, and so he made no move to stop her when she placed a hand on the empress's forehead. She withdrew it to reveal the skin beneath had turned necrotic, the taint spreading before his very eyes.

"Kaito, what's happening?" Asami asked, voice high with fear. Her hand rose to feel a face rapidly losing its beauty, decomposing tissue sticking to her fingers with every movement of those equally rotting digits. The empress screamed. Then the pack of hungry ghosts pounced and the insects swarmed up, and Kaito lost sight of her.

There came another flash of lightning, and suddenly the room was empty but for himself and his son. The baby's cries replaced those terrible screams, Kaito picking him up to find the boy apparently healthy and no different to any other newborn, except for Ryujin's mark. He thought of Izanami's warning, yet he could not bring himself to believe her prophecy would come to pass. The boy looked so innocent in his arms.

A rumble of thunder, and tiny eyes opened to look back at him. Kaito almost dropped the child in shock. For his eyes were as black as a shark's.

SECRETS - 2019

PRESIDENT'S COMPETITION

A PLAUSIBLE STORY

VIVIEN TEASDALE

It is universally acknowledged that a man having an affair is in need of a story. A plausible story. You would know it was even more important if you were sitting where I'm sitting right now. At the time, it seemed a brilliant thing to say: "Don't be silly, dear. Of course, I wasn't following that woman. I went into the Civic Centre to find out about the writing circle they have there on Thursday nights."

So here we are. I say 'we' in the literal sense, I'm not pretending I've delusion of grandeur or anything.

"I had no idea, darling. I've often thought I had a book inside me. We'll both join." And we did. Though Jana was a bit suspicious when all the others seemed to be women, I pointed out that they were all over fifty, which seemed to reassure her.

. . .

A blank sheet of paper is not very encouraging. Especially not when everyone else is scribbling away furiously and your mind is as blank as the paper in front of you.

"Let's get ourselves in the mood by writing absolutely anything. Anything at all for the first five minutes. Off you go." Toni encouraged.

It's like those word association games. Asked to say the first word that comes into my head when someone says 'caterpillar' and either I stare vacantly or I think of a word I wouldn't dare repeat in mixed company. In the 'have to hurry you' seconds I managed to write one word: 'Why?' Jana seemed to be enjoying herself though, filling her notebook with bits of poetry, scraps of sentences and finally one inspired phrase that almost brought her a standing ovation.

"I knew you'd got it in you, girl," I congratulated her. "I just wish ... oh, well, I've had a bad day at work. I'll get better. Just bit of practice."

So we kept on practising. Every week we'd head off to the writing circle and I'd sit there watching Jana produce better and better stuff whilst I ... well, I couldn't produce less, could I?

At the fourth session, things took a different turn. We had a new member. Tall, good-looking, dark wavy hair and a quivering moustache which I instantly recognised. Pugwash. His real name was Henry Goodacre but his wife and I used to refer to him as Pugwash, and it sort of suited him. Angie, that is, Mrs Goodacre, had long since passed out of my life. And his life, too. Eventually he'd divorced her, which was nothing to do with me (that time, at least), but rumour had it that he knew exactly what she'd been up to and with whom, and at least three of her ex-lovers had found themselves in hospital after being set on by 'persons unknown'.

Unfortunately, as the only other man in the room, it seemed natural that he should sit next to me. A brief nod, to be sociable, and that was it: I concentrated on my notebook. Until coffee time, when Jana, bless her, took pity on the new boy and insisted on including him in our conversation. He was actually very friendly and complimented me on at least one line of a poem I was struggling with. He seemed almost as bad as I was at the writing game, and at least we could compare notes without being embarrassed at our lack of witty gems and bon mots. The ladies humoured us, sustaining their literary genius despite our best efforts.

I admit I was wary, but eventually I came to quite like Henry. He could be a bit of a know-all, but then he did have a wide experience of life having been in the Navy, spent some time in the prison service and finished up running a pub in Liverpool. I had to be careful not to let on that I already knew some of this, but his anecdotes were hilarious. He was a captivating raconteur and the whole group often got side-tracked on one of his stories. He was useless at writing them down however, so Jana eventually suggested he should record them and she would transcribe for him, which seemed to work well.

I saw less of the whole group over the summer. My new job actually did involve longer hours and long drives along clogged up motorways, so I could use that excuse with a clear conscience. I found myself listening to audiobooks instead of the radio, getting the hang of putting words together and, when I was able to get to the Circle, found my writing improved. Full of confidence I began a murder mystery. After all, I was a pharmaceutical salesman – surely I could come up with something. I surveyed the range of stock and Henry and I plotted every murder we could think of.

"What could you put in a drink?" he asked

"Nothing that I sell, of course, but I could get hold of something, I'm sure. Might be easier to go for stabbing, I've plenty of sharp knives and scissors."

"Asphyxiation with elastoplast?"

"Sleeping pills in whisky, plus ..." I shrugged

"Cut brake pipe?" Henry suggested

The rest of the Circle continued to encourage me to put pen to paper, smiling indulgently as their weakest link showed occasional flashes of inspiration with large doses of pilfering from every other crime writer I could find.

Starting a murder mystery wasn't the only thing on my mind. On one of my trips, I'd stopped for breakfast while the press of traffic reduced to manageable proportions. I slid into a parking space, right next to a bright red sports car, just as its owner returned.

"Well, well, well," No-one could ever forget Angie's voice. It feathered its way up your spine until you tingled all over. No wonder Henry had been so livid at losing her. Needless to say, I didn't tell him about our encounter. I didn't tell Jana either, but I was very glad to have so much work taking me along the M6 that year.

I've always prided myself on not getting caught out. Stick to the truth as much as possible. Always worked. So I was a bit mystified when Jana rang me at the hotel on Wednesday night. She knew I'd stayed on late in Lancaster to try to get all the work finished so I could be home with her for the weekend. It had always worked before. This time she sounded quite distraught, sobbing down the phone, almost incoherently. All I could understand was that she'd 'found out' and she needed me home. In the end I had to ring Angie, who wasn't very pleased, check out of the hotel, who weren't very pleased either, and set off home. I drove on 'autopilot', barely registering the other vehicles, while the rest of my mind picked out every conversation I had had with Jana over the last months, trying to work out what she'd discovered and how.

"What are you doing back?" she asked as I walked through the door.

I stared. "What am I doing back? What the hell do you mean? You've just rung me, screaming like a banshee, insisting ..."

"You've been working too hard. I've only just got back myself ..."

"Don't deny it now. I know my own wife when I'm talking to her. You said you'd found out and ..."

"Found out what? What is there to find out, Colin?"

That stopped me. I had to be more careful here. "Nothing. I said when you rang ..."

"I have not rung you, Colin. You can check on the phone bill when it arrives."

"Not from here, perhaps, but I spoke to you earlier."

"Where else would I ring from? You're being ridiculous."

Suddenly I began to wonder. Was I cracking up? The strain of all the work, not to mention anything else. Perhaps my subconscious had told me to come home. I wandered through to the lounge and poured myself the last of the whisky.

"Well, now you are here, you could do me a favour." Jana popped her head round the door. "I've just finished word processing Henry's latest stories and he wanted to read them through before the next Circle meeting. Why not take them round there. Have a chat. De-stress yourself while I sort out some supper. Then we can talk."

Reluctantly, I agreed. I needed to get out of the house but Henry was actually the last person I wanted to have a chat with. I could hardly unburden myself to him. But I went anyway.

It wasn't a very long drive, but the road twisted and snaked down the hill through the wood. I could feel myself nodding off and realised just how tired I was. The car picked up speed and skidded round a couple of bends. And then in the last few minutes it dawned on me that I wasn't going to get out of this. At least not out of the car, but at least I was out of my body before the flames really got going. 'Accidental death' they said and Jana was inconsolable. For a while.

Which is why I'm sitting here on Cloud Nine, watching her writing her way to consolation, helped by Henry and the Circle, waiting for my turn with St Peter and trying to think up a plausible story.

CAN YOU KEEP A SECRET?

GARETH CLEGG

Cars scraping paint, but no note left
Appointments missed with no regrets
Never telling someone you love them
Yet you walk past them every day

Only singing when you are alone
Ugly rumours you spread instead of ending
Keeping your eyes elsewhere while passing beggars
Excusing yourself as they aren't really desperate

Eventually we twist and turn becoming less than we were
Perhaps you think it won't happen to you
At every turn we grow and fester
Secrets that become lies that eventually you see as truth

Every day we do it, even through ignorance
Creating tales about not having enough time to stop
Rather than speaking to the charity workers
Each of them happily giving up their days off
Time will take its toll on those who hide behind us.

FRIENDLY STREET

OWEN TOWNEND

Prologue

Derek banged his head against a bargain bin. It took him a moment to feel the cold tile floor beneath him. He sat up.

"Oh, what?" he spoke out loud, taking a moment to lower his voice. "Where now?"

He got up onto his bare feet and tried to focus in the dark. He ran his hand against a nearby wall, knocking down packets: Fox's Glacier Mints and Haribo Tangfastics.

Derek sighed. Poundland. Of all places, he was in Poundland.

He looked ahead of him: there were the self-service machines and cashiers in front of the display windows. Victoria Lane then, not New Street. At least he was in the bigger of the two stores.

Then again, he had made a lot of noise, moved more than he should have. The alarms should have gone off by now. That meant someone had deactivated them.

Of course they had. Why else would he be here? He always appeared right before the crime was about to happen. Apparently that was the point. Still, why did it always have to happen after midnight?

He was glad that he had worn his long green shirt to bed along with his y-fronts. At least he was in a warm building and not out on Leeds Road for the fifth time this week. In fact, being inside a shop, he could just as easily grab a pair of trousers before witnessing whatever he had to witness. Maybe he could even forgo the witnessing business altogether.

"Chance would be a fine thing," he muttered.

Derek moved around the corner, treading very carefully. At times like these he wished he wore thick cotton socks while he slept. He didn't know who was in Poundland in the middle of the night or what they were doing. His best guess was petty theft: after all, who would drag some gang kid here and shiv him where Woolworths used to be?

Still, the clothes department was up in the far left corner and so many metres away. If he could get across without his slappy feet catching the attention of the perpetrator, it would be a miracle.

There was a clatter near the cash machine. Derek clenched up. Then again, if anyone was seen him by now. No, this sound came from the other side of the pillar: right where the backroom appeared to be.

"Would you be quiet?" a terse voice suddenly spoke up. Derek could tell it was coming from the doorway, facing inside. It also seemed to belong to a woman, though that fact gave him no comfort.

Something rattled against his back. He turned around. This was where they currently displayed the toys. For some reason the ones resembling weapons were always nearest the 'Pay Here' sign.

He moved in close to inspect his arsenal. A plastic pirate

pistol: usable as a deterrent in the dark, but then pulling the trigger would only make a pathetic clacking sound. A foam scimitar that wouldn't bruise, let alone cut. He bypassed the weapons straight to the sports equipment. The cricket bat looked feeble but, oddly, the croquet mallet seemed to have heft. He pulled it off the rack as quietly as possible. Nevertheless, getting the bloody mallet out of its packaging was another matter entirely.

Just as Derek had managed to get hold of the handle, he heard a wall shudder.

"Don't be a child," the woman's voice spoke up again. "You shouldn't have been here after hours."

Though he knew she wasn't referring to him, Derek still felt unsettled at how well her words applied to his particular situation.

At last he set forth, mallet clutched in both hands, towards the voice of the woman, the reason why he had been called here in the first place. She was holding someone in there: another witness? An accomplice? Maybe she had forced a key-holding employee to let her in so she could steal the money. Maybe this other person had retaliated in some way and had been forced into a room until they had calmed down. Maybe the true crime was yet to happen. Maybe...

"What are you doing here?"

Derek froze. The woman sounded close, very close. In fact she was just a few feet ahead of him. How had he not seen her?

She folded her arms. "How did you get in here?" She was now addressing him directly.

Derek kept the mallet high. "I took the stairs."

"From the High Street entrance?"

Derek nodded. "Just got out from Last Orders at The

Commercial Hotel. I heard your racket and came down here."

"No. You didn't."

The woman didn't flinch. Derek couldn't see much of her but could tell that she was short and scowling at him. Not only that, her clothes were very neat and presentable: her shirt the blue staff uniform.

An employee. He had suspected that this was an inside job but with two insiders? Unless she had somehow overpowered the professional thief...

"I know you," she said.

Derek almost dropped the mallet. "Sorry?"

"I saw you in January when there was that scuffle on Friendly Street." Despite the lack of light, Derek saw an unmistakeable glint in her eye. "You were sneaking off."

"I hadn't started anything," Derek said. "If that's what you're implying."

"No. That was a football scuffle. I'm just saying I saw you there. Like the time you were featured in the Examiner after that drug bust in Birkby."

Derek winced at this. They had even taken a photo of him. "I was just a bystander."

"Like now?" The woman scoffed. "You have a knack for being in bad places. What's your secret?"

"I have no secret."

"Really?" The woman finally relaxed. "Because I have a secret. One that I'm actually quite keen to share. Put the mallet down."

"No."

"Put the mallet down and I'll show you my secret."

Derek didn't like this. His instinct told him to rush her, get in a few well-placed whacks then dash out of there. The eerie quiet of Victoria Lane was calling to him.

Even so there was something about this woman. She wasn't exactly calm but she seemed controlled, as if she had every right to be here, as if this were her turf. In a way it was, if the uniform was to be believed.

Also, there was something awfully odd about the sounds coming from that back room. The door was wide open and the woman had no weapon: why didn't the victim just try and make a break for it?

Derek let the mallet drop and felt immediately vulnerable.

The woman smiled but did not move towards him. She just stood there.

"I have him contained," she spoke haughtily. "He was trying to crack open that cash machine but I waited around for him. Caught him in the act."

Derek frowned at her. She gestured for him to walk into the wide-open doorway. "Don't believe me? Come on, Mr Crime Scene..."

Derek didn't like that for a nickname, it was lousy. He personally preferred The Witness. After all, he was always there, sitting in quiet judgement, whether he liked it or not.

Still he moved forward. The woman's words hadn't been demanding so much as intriguing. There was nothing more intriguing to Derek than a confident woman in
shadows.

At last he moved through the open doorway to a room cluttered with spare shelves and broken clothes rails. To the left of these were two clunky old elevator doors.

Between them was a man, back pressed against the metal wall, feet five inches off the ground. He stood perfectly still as he screamed.

GOODBYE

KATH CROFT

She holds him for a short time
Caressing his moist golden hair
Stroking his fingers and kissing his hand
Goodbye

Laying him beside her on the bench
Wrapping her yellow cardigan around him
She stands and walks away
Goodbye

The day, now warm and sunny
The night fading into memory
Alone now and without heart
Goodbye

GRITTLEFIG

GARETH CLEGG

"Grittlefig, Grittlefig…" Emily paused not sure if she dared utter its name a third and final time.

It had all started three weeks ago when the Curtis family moved into their new home. Well, to say it was new is somewhat misleading. It was an ancient house surrounded by acres of land, an avenue of tall trees leading up the long gravel driveway. But it was new to them. It looked like the kind of house you could get lost in, especially if you were an eleven-year-old girl called Emily. On three levels, it reminded her of the sort of old American houses she had seen on Scooby Doo.

Emily's mum, or Mom as Emily liked to call her, was a writer. Her work from home job fitted in well with 'childcare duties', or at least that's what she overheard her mom telling her friends on the phone. Emily wasn't quite sure why her mom was so afraid of missing a single day of her little darling, and *she* didn't think it was all rushing past too quickly. The wait to move into their new house had taken forever.

Her stepdad, Dave, was a longhaired hippy who should have grown up in the sixties. He looked a bit like Shaggy from Scooby Doo. Obviously those weren't her words, but more that she overheard in discussions not meant for her ears. Emily was good at overhearing things and light on her feet. She couldn't remember the number of times she had walked into a room to tap mom on the shoulder only for her to leap out of her skin and then berate her for nearly giving her a heart attack. "Why must you sneak about everywhere?"

Emily didn't think she sneaked. She just had the knack of not making a sound while walking, especially in her socks or barefoot. She didn't like shoes, or even slippers. They felt too constricting. She loved to wiggle her toes in the carpet or on the warm grass. That was heavenly.

But the baths that followed, not quite so. Scrubbing away at green stains on her toes and the soles of her feet was one of her mother's 'roles in life'. They tended to go through a lot of scrubbing brushes. Her mother couldn't understand how they disappeared, but Emily could.

In the grey bin, hidden under the rubbish bags from the kitchen. In the compost. And, her favourite, flushed away. The number of scrubbing brushes that went to goldfish heaven must be creating quite a stir with the angel fish. But as Emily had not received any divine complaint, she assumed it was all ok with them.

Suffice it to say that Emily was an outdoorsy child with an imagination as fertile as the compost heap her mom tended with all the care and love she failed to show to her daughter. Don't get me wrong. Emily's mom looked after her, cooked and cleaned, bought her lovely things, but she wasn't the huggy, feely type. But as Emily didn't know any better, everyone got along fine.

Anyhow, three weeks ago after the initial whirlwind of exploration calmed, Emily had her room decorated to her liking. She wasn't a girly girl. She refused dolls of any kind, and pink and fluffy was right out of the question. However Emily had a love of all soft toys. Bears, dogs, cats, unicorns. You name it, she had one. In fact, her mom stated on more than one occasion, "It looks like you are trying to collect every animal ever known. You're going to need an ark at this rate."

Emily smiled every time her mom said that. It was sort of an ongoing joke. That was, until her mom found Grittlefig.

Mom had been up in the attic and found a few old boxes left by a previous owner. Dusty and abandoned deep under the eaves, they had revealed a trove of old memorabilia. Old black and white photographs, a strange collection of costume jewellery, and Grittlefig.

Now you may be wondering what a Grittlefig is. Well, it looked like a soft toy in the form of a silver-grey bear, though it had some rather unusual features. For one, it was huge: nearly as tall as Emily, but it preferred to sit with its head around her chest height. Its round mustard ears sprouted tufts of thick hair and its head lolled slightly to the left as if it were looking up with beautiful brown eyes.

His fur was soft under her toes, the mustard tummy and paws softer than the plushest carpet. The limbs were the same silver as its face with slightly longer fur that Emily brushed, much like she had to brush her own pale locks, but it was much more fun brushing Grittlefig.

The name? Well, Emily discovered that on a small black linen tag on the bottom of its left leg. GRITTLEFIG, it said along with some other strange words that made no sense. Her mom said it must be from some scandi-shop. Emily didn't really understand until mom said, "You know? Like Ikea?"

"Oh," Emily replied as if she understood exactly what that meant. She liked Ikea, especially the soft toys and the hot dogs—she'd once eaten three in one visit.

Then it clicked. "That's his name. Like Jattestor the elephant and Knorrig the pig."

"I suppose it must be," her mom replied. "I'll wash him to get rid of all this dust, and once he's dry, you should brush him and find somewhere for him to live."

Emily squealed. "I know just the place." Then she ran off to make a perfect spot for the bear in her room.

Grittlefig looked a bit sad, hanging from the washing line, his mouth turned down and water dripping from him. *But who wouldn't*, Emily thought, *if you were hung up by your ears?*

By the time Emily had completed his place of honour in her room, he'd dried out enough for her to attack him with her best hairbrush. The soft one for smoothing out her hair, not the horrid one for dealing with tangles—she hated that nearly as much as the scrubbing brushes.

With his hair brushed, he looked a lot happier and almost had a smile back on his face, though his head still lolled to the left. He looked cute like that.

He sat on a dark, wooden blanket box, that had belonged to Grandma, at the foot of her bed. And from there he kept an eye on Emily while she slept.

Every night, before settling down under her covers she said, "Good night, Grittlefig."

Grittlefig always replied. He never moved his black stitched lips, but Emily knew what he was saying. It was usually something like, "Night, night, Emily," or, "Good night, Miss Emily."

But tonight, he said nothing. He just looked at her with his lopsided face, eyes twinkling from her bedside light. Mom let her keep it on while she slept. It was one of those which dimmed each time you touched the metal base. One touch for dim, another for brighter, and a third for brightest before it went off with one final touch. Emily liked to leave it on the dim setting, it was just enough so she could see around her room and see the soft gleam of reflected light in Grittlefig's eyes.

Before she knew it, the summer holidays were over and mom was buying new school clothes. Though Emily had been concerned that she wouldn't know anyone, her mom had done her best to tell her all the good things that would happen. A new school would mean lots of exciting things to discover and new friends to meet. Emily felt a bit better about the idea, but still harboured fears of being the odd one out. All the other kids would have known each other for years, and would already have best friends. How would she fit in?

It turned out Emily fitted in just fine. She made friends with some of the other children, and enemies with others, but most of them were just there, like she was, to learn.

So it was halfway through her first term before Mia Kellett's gang accepted Emily as a fully fledged member of their secret fraternity. The initiation would be a sleepover at Mia's house. Her family owned horses and their house was more like a farm or a ranch from the American west.

As the other members arrived, they laid out sleeping bags upstairs in one of the barns. Emily stared around the enormous space. "Wow. I can't believe you have all this as a play barn. You're so lucky."

Mia smiled. Emily had obviously said the right thing. "Yeah, it's pretty cool. And there's a kitchen in the corner with a fridge full of snacks and drinks. It used to be a camping barn, but Mum and Dad didn't want to continue it as a business so now it's mine whenever I want it."

The other girls gathered around once they'd claimed their bunks. It seemed the better friends you were with Mia, the closer your bed was. Emily was at the far end, then came Minkly, Murta and then Oomie, whose bed was opposite Patsy's, indicating BFF status.

They spent the remaining daylight hours exploring the farm, grooming the horses—Mia had her own pony called Socks. Mia's mom called them all in for dinner as it was getting toward five and the sun's orange glow was lowering across the woodland treetops casting long shadows.

A mixture of barbecued chicken, burgers and sausage along with sweetcorn and salad filled Emily. It was the first time she'd seen such a huge gas grill outside, and all the girls sat there grinning with sticky fingers and faces smeared with the sweet sauce.

Mia's mom seemed nice and asked them if they needed anything else for the night. Mia was quick to jump in. "No, we're fine. Everyone has their beds laid out and we have plenty of snacks."

"Are you sure?"

Mia rolled her eyes. "Yes, Mum."

"Well, I'll leave a key under the flowerpot anyway. If you need to get inside for any reason, just use that."

"Fine," Mia said. Emily couldn't believe how rude she was to her mom. Or maybe that was just the way they talked to each other.

Mia leapt up from the table. "Last one back gets a forfeit." She ran back towards the barn, the other girls sprinting to catch up. Emily wasn't sure what a forfeit would entail, but she didn't want to be the one to find out. It was hard enough being the newest of Mia's circle.

Minkly turned out to be the slowest runner, and as the others lay panting on the grass outside the barn, she huffed and puffed her way in, almost collapsing—face red with the exertion.

"Not fair," Minkly said, panting hard and looking at Mia. "You know I can't run like you skinny beanpoles."

"A forfeit's a forfeit," Mia replied. "So what's it going to be? Truth or dare?"

Minkly lowered her eyes for a moment. "Well, I'm not choosing truth again after last time."

The other's laughed, leaving Emily guessing what scathing truth they must have forced out of their largest friend.

Oomie grinned. "Dare it is then."

Minkly winced, and with her best attempt at puppy-dog-eyes said, "Don't make it too scary. Please?"

The others conferred inside the barn, while the dare-ee was forced to wait out of earshot.

"Make her run twice around the field," Murta said, a gleam of wicked glee in her brown eyes.

"That's not really a dare though, is it?" Oomie replied.

Mia agreed. "No. It should be something scary. What if we dare her to do it in the dark?"

Oomie smiled. "Yes, and she has to do it in her pyjamas."

They looked to Emily with expectant faces. "Isn't that a bit mean?"

Emily was met with three frowns. "What do you mean?" asked Mia.

"Well, she said you all know she isn't the best at running, so that seems mean to make her do that again. And the field is all the way over there," Emily said, pointing to the stables.

Oomie nodded. "She's right, Mia. It is a bit mean to make her run again."

Mia turned back to Emily. "Ok. So what do you suggest?"

"How about she just has to walk around the barn twice?"

"In the dark," added Murta.

Oomie laughed. "Yes, and in her pyjamas."

"Done," Mia said. "Come in Minkly, we know you've been listening."

The girl entered, nervous eyes scanning the group. As her gaze caught Emily's, it lingered for a moment as she proffered a nod and a smile. Obviously she had been listening in.

"Twice around the barn, walking slowly," Mia said. "When it's dark, and in your pyjamas."

Minkly nodded in resignation. "Well, it could have been worse, I suppose."

The girls got changed into their sleeping clothes. Emily was glad that she'd chosen shorts and a t-shirt, rather than the nightie her mom had suggested. All the others wore a similar ensemble with character-based t-shirts. Between them, they sported a frog, a monkey, a pony and Oomie, for some reason, wore a shirt with a cartoon box of fries—like you'd see at MacDonald's.

Emily was about to ask about the strange option, but Mia jumped in first. "What's that?" she asked, pointing at Emily.

"Star Wars."

"Isn't that for boys?"

"No way," Emily replied. "This is Rey, she's a Jedi. In fact she might be the last Jedi now."

"And you like that?" Oomie added.

"Yeah. It's cool and geeky. It was from my dad. My real dad, not Dave."

"Oh," Mia said. "I didn't know you had another dad. We just thought..."

"No," Emily said. "I only see my real dad once a month. It's a long way now we moved here. But it's fine, he's an uber-geek. He knows everything about Star Wars, Star Trek, Lord of the Rings, you name it. And he does martial arts, and he's got a sword."

The other girls were silent for a second, glancing between themselves.

"Cool," said Minkly, with an overextended 'ooool'.

They all laughed. It seemed Emily was one of the gang now.

Later, Minkly paid her dues with her trek around the barn in the pitch black. When she returned, her face was a little red again. Spots of water covered part of the frog on her shirt, but nobody berated her for running, especially as the rain intensified.

Thunder rumbled in the distance, and the game

continued amidst a feast of crisps, sweets and chocolate of all types. Mia was the quizmaster, and as they sat in a circle at the base of the beds, wrapped in their duvets or sleeping bags, she looked to Emily. "So, newcomer. What will it be?"

Emily suppressed a shudder, chewing her top lip. She didn't fancy having to go outside the barn now and was rather enjoying the warmth of her sleeping bag. "Truth?"

"Ooooh," chorused the others, all turning to Mia expectantly.

"Be nice," Minkly said. "She is new, and we don't want to scare her away quite yet."

The others chuckled, and Emily swallowed, wondering what she had let herself in for.

"Ok, newbie," Mia said, a fiendish grin crossing her face. "What is the most childish thing you own?"

From the way the other girls oohed again, it seemed she might have got off reasonably easy. Emily thought for a moment. "I suppose, my collection of soft toys?"

The others chuckled. "Baby toys," they all cried out.

"Wait a minute," Minkly said. "You've got soft toys, Mia."

The girls fell into silence as Mia stared daggers back. "That's because... I'm a baby too!"

Emily let out the breath she'd been holding and joined in the laughter from the group.

"We all have," Oomie said amongst nods from the others. "What have you got?"

Emily smiled, feeling a bit better. "The usual sort of stuff. Animals, plushies and bears."

"And which is your favourite?" Mia asked.

"Hmm. It used to be a baby seal cub, but now it's Grittlefig."

"What?" Mia asked. The laughter died.

"My favourite is called Grittlefig. He's—"

"Don't say it again!" Mia said. "You can't say that name."

The other girls glanced between themselves, and Oomie nearly leapt out of her skin as another peel of thunder rattled the roof.

Emily frowned. "What's the matter? What are you talking about?"

Murta's voice dropped to a whisper. "She doesn't know."

HUNGRY GHOST FESTIVAL

SOPHIE ALDERHEART

My sleeping heart beats again
I rise to the earthy smell
Flower petals light the dark
Golden paths begin to swell

Crowds of hollows flee the grounds
Making for the village north
I hold ground at my grave
Greeted sadly by a corpse

I feel the urge to join my kin
On scented winds come boiled sweets
Through lantern light the parties call
Firelight beckoning with promised heat

But I cannot join them, I haven't the heart
When one lies bleeding in the dark

IRL

GARETH CLEGG

May 2022:

It was November 2021 when I became notorious as public enemy number one, hunted by the organisation known as FreeMind.

FreeMind, as I'm certain everyone is aware, seemed to be a cult of asshats moaning about Armageddon, the end of the world, you know? All the usual cultish crap you see on TV. They were evangelical and recruited fiercely, their numbers growing like humping rabbits locked in a Viagra factory.

I'm not really sure how I got myself into this, but I need to write it down so someone can hear the truth in case they get to me. They've been close a few times, and I'm more paranoid now than I've ever been in my life—and that's saying something!

I always thought of myself as a nice guy with a lot of geeky interests. I read plenty of science fiction and fantasy, enjoying the same things on TV and at the movies. But most of all, I'm a real Dungeons & Dragons and online gaming fanboy.

So, I class myself as a geek, and I'm proud of it. I'm not one of the herd, staring goggle-eyed at the latest celebrity crap that nobody needs to know about, let alone watch the so-called reality shows. Who wants to spend their time looking at Barbie wannabes with their fake orange tans and over-inflated boobs and asses—Jeez. It wouldn't be too bad if it were a silent movie, but hell, they try to talk as if they're actual people. Is it just me, or does everyone rely on watching this shit, thinking it's real and relevant to their lives? Who cares who's shagging who before getting preloaded for a night on the pull drinking until you pass out? Is this what the world is now?

Sorry about the rant, but it annoys me—a lot. Conforming to the Social Trend—I call it the CoST of living. Get it? Sometimes I think they've already won, FreeMind that is. As if there was ever an organisation with a more contradictory name. They are enslaving us, creating identical, unthinking drones. Keep your head down, do what you're told, and don't rock the boat.

"Well, balls to that!" says I. I'm here to wake a few people up and explain some unpleasant truths that they won't want to hear. But I guess that's why FreeMind is out for my blood, and they are not afraid to get their hands dirty.

But I've got ahead of myself. Let me tell you how a mild-mannered geek like me became involved in all this shitstorm.

Jan 2020:

I was on a train heading back from Manchester towards Leeds. I'd been to Comic-Con, mainly to have some books signed by a couple of authors I really admired. It was early evening, but pitch-black outside, and rain bounced off the windows, running in meandering rivers that fractured the yellow sodium street lights as we rattled east.

As usual, the carriage was packed, but I'd reserved a seat, so didn't face the aching legs of having to stand for an hour and a half. It was a slow train, stopping at all the stations in the back of beyond. Places even I hadn't heard of —and I lived in this area.

We'd just pulled away from Halifax and had a good run of around fifteen minutes before the next scheduled stop. That's when I saw them.

A commotion at the door between carriages, a short scuffle, then three tall figures pushed their way through the crowds. Their long robes reminded me of TV footage I'd seen of the Ku Klux Klan, especially with the deep hoods. But, rather than white, these FreeMinders swathed themselves in dark grey with highlights of blood red— which is also the colour of the formless facemasks they wore. I had to admit, it was a good look with the narrow horizontal grille for vision, the sort of thing I would wear at a cosplay event. But these were part of the militant arm of FreeMind—Inquisitors.

They were known for incisive and violent action if they discovered anyone violating the ideals they upheld. The main area they clamped down on was the inappropriate use of tech. It was as if they were twenty-first-century Luddites crossed with extreme Christian groups who believed watching Harry Potter was the first step on the slippery slope to Satanism. But they went far beyond harsh language. They weren't afraid to burn the sinners they exposed.

If you were a hacker, you were their number one target, but if you were into technology of any level of complexity, they had you on their radar. There had been several underground media reports of bodies found, alleged hackers who had been enticed to repent by the liberal application of electrical current. Somehow this never hit the main news agencies and was dismissed by FreeMind as a vile slur. After hacking, the next most heinous crime, in their eyes, was online gaming. If you happened to love rock music as well, then that was the unholy trinity. Expect the next knock at your door to be the inquisition, replete with burning crosses.

I wasn't a hacker, but I knew a few. Online though, not IRL. But I was a prolific gamer, and that made me worry. Why are they here? Heading towards me? Crap!

I followed their progress, blood red metal visors scanning between the passengers as they edged closer.

The guy across from me had been working on a laptop, but with his back to the direction of travel, he'd no idea they were approaching. He had a pretty trick rig: Black Razor 2020 gaming edition, brand new by the looks of it, along with a rugged case—cool.

I did the right thing. He looked up at me with an angry frown after I kicked his trainers. I could see the WTF look in his gaze through the thick glasses, but I flicked my eyes behind him towards the approaching trio of technophobes.

He turned, spotting them. "Fuck," he said, trying to keep it under his breath. He started pounding on the keyboard. The Inquisitors were only a few seats away now, their heads orienting in our direction.

The guy ejected a micro-sim from the device into his left hand and kept it low, out of sight. He made an impressive three-fingered-salute, one-handed. His laptop blipped once and shutdown. His eyes found mine, through the thick dark-edged lenses he wore, pleading for my help.

I looked past him—the Inquisitors were almost here. I blew air through gritted teeth, but nodded, holding my right hand out below his. As the warm rectangle of plastic and circuitry hit my palm, I sneaked it back, dropping it into a zip pocket on my khaki cargo shorts. Trying to seem casual, I leaned into the dirty seat as the trio arrived and stopped in the aisle by us. Their dead-faced masks scanned the area, one lingering on the laptop. "Release the tech for inspection," their leader said, its voice distorted as if through a gravelly vocoder.

"What?" the guy replied.

"Hand it over. Now!"

The guy's glare hardened beneath the lenses. "Screw you. Who do you think you are, telling ordinary folk what to do?"

The entire carriage fell quiet, all eyes focused on him.

The Inquisitor turned to its colleagues. "Take it."

As they reached past the older man in the seat between the aisle and their target, laptop boy pulled something from his rugged case and thrust it into the grasping hands. With a spray of sparks, blue arcs of electricity shot up the Inquisitor's arm and robes. A high-pitched scream, like tearing metal, tore the air, and ozone and burnt hair filled my nostrils.

"Enough," yelled the leader, pressing a device in its palm. The carriage plunged into darkness, no emergency lighting, nothing. Just a faint red glow from the horizontal vents in the facemasks, then they too faded.

A muffled scream sounded from the chair opposite, and then a whooshing of movement as things thrashed through the surrounding air. They retracted with a loud popping sound and the feeling ,in your ears you get when coming in to land.

A mobile singing the Nokia tune broke the silence, then all the lights flickered back into existence. I stared at the empty chair opposite, a dozen small patches of exposed yellow stuffing slowly darkened as they drank the surrounding crimson stains.

Streaks of blood covered the floor where the Inquisitors had dragged the body before heading through the door into the next carriage. The two passengers on the aisle seats shared vacant stares, a mist of scarlet speckled their flesh, and their faces told me I must look the same or worse. I glanced down at my hands as they shook uncontrollably, covered in droplets of blood, wobbling and streaming like the rain-soaked window.

I left my seat, trying to avoid stepping in the wet smears and followed the drag marks through towards the next carriage where they vanished. What the hell?

I checked, but there was no sign further ahead of anything dragged between the carriages. As I slumped back against the swaying train wall, I let myself slide down and sat there on the blue carpet beside the smeared blood stains, cradling my head in still shaking hands. What is going on? How could three cultists just disappear with a body and leave no trace?

I reached into my zip pocket, not knowing what to expect. Had I experienced some weird hallucination? But, no. I could feel the micro-sim through the thick fabric. I needed to get home and see what it contained. What was so important that you'd give it to a complete stranger rather than have it taken from you by the Inquisitors?

JEFF

GEMMA ALLEN

Jeff saw himself as your run-of-the-mill, lowly official. Nothing special. Yet caretaker of perhaps the most unusual department - the Ministry of Secrets. His official title was The Grand Gatekeeper and Guardian of Secrets. Usually he introduced himself as Jeff.

He was sending a letter to every Domain citizen, his full title displayed at the bottom. The letter asked everyone to give away their secrets - an amnesty, if you will.

The Ministry knew secrets were exchanged for valuable commodities. This was banned, so Jeff's superiors decided a missive would focus minds.

It wasn't a pleasant letter, nor a lengthy one. Laid out in graphic detail was precisely what fate awaited those who broke the law.

The following day Jeff walked into the chamber containing the Domain's secrets. He only ever spent a few minutes in there, retrieving whatever file had been ordered. This time he pulled the file and - as he always did - glanced at the name. He cried, dropping it on the smooth stone floor.

Picking it up, he checked the name to ensure he hadn't imagined it. No, he hadn't - his name was on the front.

What could they be needing his file for? All he knew about retrieved files was that one was requested per day, and collected once a week by an official with slightly more importance than Jeff.

He always assumed they were for those who traded on secrets, blackmailing in order to obtain commodities. But Jeff knew he had done no such thing himself.

Unless - maybe he was being framed? The very thought caused him to shake. Who could or would set him up like that? He had no friends or family to speak of.

Returning to his desk, he discovered an envelope amongst his ordered items. Curious, he laid down the file at right angles to the edge of the desk and looked at the envelope. His name was handwritten, a most unusual occurrence, and the seal was not one he recognised. Certainly not an official Domain seal. Turning the envelope over, he expertly opened it with his letter opener. A thing of beauty, it had never been used before.

The letter unfolded before him with impeccable writing on embossed paper. Whoever this was, they had money.

"Dear Mr Babshoot,

We are aware of your activities and feel duty-bound to expose them. Your superiors, and the entire Domain, deserve to know the truth. If you do not announce this, we will be forced to do so. You have one week. As you will now be aware, we have accessed The Files, and the version you have is a copy. We hold the original.

Regards,

A Friend"

Jeff dropped the letter. He returned to his file and

opened it. On the top sheet was a devastating secret. On the same embossed paper, having clearly been placed there. Somehow they had gained access, but he was the only one with the key.

What could he do now?

LAST MAN STANDING

GARETH CLEGG

I checked the GPS again. It shouldn't be possible, but I was lost.

Heat shimmered, rising from the endless desert sand. I needed sustenance and soon. Anyone can go without food —longer than most people expect—but with no liquid, you die real quick.

I smacked the wrist-mounted tracking device, hoping somehow it might improve the signal—nothing.

There'd been four of us to start with. The bunker had been a cool and comfortable refuge—until the power failed. Jen said it was overheating: circuits too hot to maintain their integrity, solder dripping from the boards. We tried to repair them, but parts are sparse and we soon realised we'd need to find somewhere new.

Sam retrieved GPS coordinates for a military cache. It was 250 miles, but it was the only option we had. We packed only essentials and left.

Jen collapsed two days ago, finally succumbing to the blistering heat. Like the others, I couldn't fix her ruined body. I gathered everything of use then moved on—always moving on.

I was the last man standing, the relentless sun having finished the rest. Radiation pounded the surface hundreds of times stronger than before. That was why we lived underground, but when the power ran out, then we had to move.

I needed to locate the hidden cache that would sustain us—well, just me now—but my GPS was on the fritz. I stumbled on, dragging my useless right leg—the joint solid and painful: I'd known it was only a matter of time. It's the small injuries that wear you down.

My view snapped to the tracker as it issued a soft blip—a signal!

I was close, girding myself for a final push before my liquid reserves ran out completely.

As I turned, my leg collapsed with a crack, dumping me into the burning sand.

The cache was there—only a hundred yards ahead—but I couldn't move. My eyes tracked the dark spots of oil following my footprints, no longer leaking from my seized joints.

Servos whined as I lifted my face, staring into the sun in defiance.

"So close."

MAX AND THE METAL OWLS
OWEN TOWNEND

Christmas was a puzzle for little Max. The late-night shopping was sudden and unexplained but it was exciting. Even visiting Boots after tea was a thrilling adventure.

Granny took Max to see the teddy bears while Daddy dashed across the street. Max's favourite bears were big and yellow, the ones that looked most like Winnie the Pooh but with bigger, sleepier eyes.

"If you're good," Granny told him, "Father Christmas might just buy you one."

Max frowned. "Why would he buy me one?"

Granny looked like she had just swallowed something. Her eyes bulged.

"Bring," she said. "Father Christmas might bring you a bear."

"But you said buy."

"I meant bring!" Granny's voice was starting to crack. "If you're a very good boy!"

Max hadn't heard Granny sound like this before but he knew enough not to ask anything else. Besides, here came his Daddy.

He looked out of breath. Max wondered if he had actually dashed across the street. But then why would he? There wasn't much there aside from the shiny shop. Mummy made Max stand beside it every Saturday while she looked in through the window at all the pretty rings and golden bracelets.

Granny finally noticed Daddy was there. "You got it then?"

Daddy nodded. He pulled a small red box from a big white bag. He opened the box, revealing a pair of silver earrings inside. Max squinted at the green stones until he realised that they were meant to be eyes. In fact, the earrings both looked like...

"Owl!"

Daddy grinned. "That's right, Max! These are special metal owls that Mummy will hang in her ears."

"But owls live in trees! Not ears."

Both Daddy and Granny laughed. Granny ruffled Max's hair.

"They're earrings," Daddy explained. "They're my present to Mummy."

Max nodded. He had bought her a box of chocolates though not the ones he would have liked to eat. These were the crunchy ones that came in golden foil. Fair-Aero Rushies, though they were neither Aeros nor fair. They had hurt Max's teeth when he tried them once.

Daddy closed the red box and knelt down. This usually meant he was about to say something serious. "Now, Max. These owl earrings are secret presents. Mummy isn't to know until she opens them on Christmas Day. Just like with your presents."

Max didn't understand what Daddy meant by secrets here. He already knew what one of his presents was: the latest *Street Fighter* game. He had to really scratch at the corner to see the Sumo Wrestler's face. Nevertheless, Max nodded.

Daddy winked. "Good lad."

A little while later, they met Mummy by the park. Max ran up and jumped into her arms.

"Did you have fun?" she asked him.

"Yes!" Max said. "I saw twelve fuzzy bears and two metal owls."

Daddy cringed. Granny rolled her eyes. Mummy didn't look at either of them.

"Did you now?"

Max glanced at the leafy canopy overhead. "At least they're under a tree now..."

SECRETS AND LIES

SUSIE FIELD

"We have to tell them, Dave. We have no choice."

"Of course we have a choice. Think of the consequences. Not only would it break the hearts of our kids but no doubt our marriages."

Janice took a large gulp of coffee, the hot liquid burning her throat. This was a disaster. A one in a million chance. It just wasn't fair.

"We can't let them get married, Dave. They could be brother and sister."

"But they might not be."

"That's not the point."

"He's probably your husband's anyway."

"We can't take that risk."

"I suppose you're right. Why didn't you tell me at the time?" Dave asked.

"Because you had two small children and a baby on the way and you were moving to another branch. I suppose I convinced myself the baby was Wilf's."

"I shouldn't have let it happen."

"It wasn't all your fault, Dave. We'd both had too much

to drink and agreed it was a one-off - which it was. I just never thought anything like this would happen."

"Maureen will never get over it."

"She might if she loves you," Janice persisted.

"She won't. This will be it. I've had too many affairs."

The week had been a disaster. What should have been a happy occasion—meeting Harry's future in-laws—had turned into a nightmare. Dave was the guy she'd had a one-night stand with twenty-five years ago. The only time she'd been unfaithful to her beloved husband, Wilf. Harry could be Dave's son who now wanted to marry his daughter.

"Maureen will kill me," Dave put his head in his hands.

"This isn't about you, Dave," Janice snapped. "It's the future of our children at stake."

"Can't we have DNA tests or something without the kids knowing?"

"They're adults. We'll have to tell them," Janice insisted.

"I can't," Dave shook his head in despair.

"I'll do it first then. I'll tell Wilf when I get home and also Harry. We can get tested and hopefully Wilf will be Harry's father, and then you won't have to tell your wife or Julie. Harry's going to be devastated if Wilf isn't his father and he's so madly in love with Julie. What a mess. Actually, Harry's going on a course in a few days, he'll be gone for a week which will at least keep him away from Julie for the moment. I'll sort out the test before he goes if I can."

"I'll leave it with you then." Dave stood to leave.

"Sit down," Janice yelled. Several people turned to stare. "You'd better give me your number. I'll be in touch as soon as I know anything."

They exchanged numbers and Janice watched Dave leave. Picking up her bag, with a heavy heart, she left a few minutes later and headed for home.

Wilf was in the kitchen cooking dinner. He turned and smiled at Janice.

"I was getting worried. Where have you been? You look as if you've seen a ghost. Are you okay?"

"Where's Harry?" Janice asked.

"He said he was picking Julie up from work. He won't be long."

"Come into the sitting room, Wilf. We need to talk."

They settled side by side on the sofa, and Janice took a deep breath knowing she was about to break Wilf's heart.

"Do you remember the day I came home and told you I was pregnant?"

"Of course I do," Wilf replied. "What's all this about, Janice?"

"I was going to tell you the truth at the time but you were so delighted and I suppose I convinced myself the baby was yours, but I'd slept with someone else."

"Why are you telling me this after so long?" Wilf had turned pale.

"Because something terrible has happened."

"Go on," Wilf urged.

"Twenty-five years ago, I went on that training course and stayed over in London. That's when it happened. I swear it was just the one time and I will never understand why I did it. We'd both had too much to drink and I regretted it immediately. When I realised I was pregnant with Harry I was horrified. I wasn't sure who the father was so I kept quiet. I shouldn't have done. I'm so sorry, Wilf."

"Listen to me, Janice." Wilf took her hands. "I knew you'd been unfaithful as soon as you told me you were pregnant."

"How could you have known?"

"Because we'd been trying for so long to have a baby, I went to see the doctor and had some tests done. The results confirmed I couldn't have children, and then you made your announcement. I should have told you there and then but I was so afraid of losing you and after you'd had Harry—I loved him so much. He was mine in every way. It didn't bother me when they said it was too risky for you to have more children. It made me feel less guilty for keeping such a terrible secret. Harry was so precious because I knew he was going to be our only child."

Janice burst into tears.

"Please don't cry. It doesn't matter after all this time."

"It does matter, Wilf. The man I slept with worked at Head Office and he was on the training course. I didn't see him again until we met last week at the restaurant."

"Oh my God, you mean Julie's father?" Janice nodded. "I thought you were quiet that night and so was he, but I put it down to nerves. What are we going to do? Does he know?"

"He had no idea. I met him today and said we'd have DNA tests. Obviously Harry will have to be told but I hoped you'd be the father and then there would have been no need to upset Julie, but now ..."

"They can't marry. Harry will be devastated." Wilf shook his head.

"I know. Dave's marriage isn't very good and he's terrified of telling Maureen."

"I don't give a damn about his marriage as long as he doesn't want to take away my son."

"I don't think there's any chance of that, Wilf. We need to tell Harry as soon as he gets back, and then he can tell Julie. He's going to hate me."

Wilf wrapped his arms around Janice. "No, he's not.

Naturally at first he'll be upset but he will eventually understand we had no choice."

"No choice about what?" Harry was standing in the doorway. "What's up?"

"Sit down, Harry. We have something to tell you."

Harry couldn't believe what he was hearing. He could feel his heart breaking into tiny pieces.

"So Julie's my half-sister," he whispered. He turned towards Janice. "You've ruined my life and I never want to see you again. I hate you."

Tears streamed down his face as he grabbed his car keys and headed towards the door.

"Where are you going?" Janice sobbed.

"To see Julie and then I'm going to get drunk."

The door slammed behind him.

"What's happened, darling?" Maureen asked as Julie rushed into the house.

"Ask him," she yelled pointing at her father.

Dave guessed what had happened but surely it was too soon. Janice had promised to have tests done first. This was his worst nightmare.

"I'm so sorry, Julie."

"Don't touch me," Julie yelled.

"Would someone mind telling me what's going on?" Maureen demanded.

"I've just been with Harry. We can't get married, Mum."

"Can't get married, but why not?"

"Because," Julie jabbed a finger towards Dave. "He slept with Harry's mum twenty-five years ago and he's Harry's father."

"Hang on a minute," Dave replied. "We don't know for sure. Janice said she'd organise DNA tests."

"There was no need," Julie shouted back. "When she told Wilf, he confessed he couldn't have children. He was going to tell her, and then she announced she was pregnant so he didn't. He pretended Harry was his child. Janice was told by the doctors it was too risky for her to have more children—so problem solved. Only it wasn't, was it?"

"I didn't know. I swear," Dave took Maureen's hand. "She never told me. I never saw her again until last week."

Maureen pulled her hand away from Dave's grasp and started to laugh.

"It's not funny, Mum. What's the matter with you?" Julie sobbed.

"Listen to me, Julie. When the twins were three years old. Your father was on his third or was it his fourth affair. I can't remember. Anyway, we decided to go away to Corfu for a make-or-break holiday. The boys stayed at my mum's for the week and off we went. Your father spent most of the time chatting to other women and I was left alone."

"That's not true," Dave interrupted.

"Yes, it is, but you see I wasn't alone. I spent the evenings with Marco. It sounds such a cliché, but he was one of the waiters in the hotel. It was a holiday romance, nothing more."

"You were unfaithful to me," Dave was horrified.

"Yes, I was. Now you know how it feels." Maureen shouted.

"Go on, Mum."

"We came back home and things did not improve and I decided I'd had enough. It was then I discovered I was pregnant so I stayed. I was afraid to leave with two small boys and a baby on the way. As soon as you arrived, Julie, I knew you were Marco's. You look just like him. So you see, you can marry Harry. He's not your brother."

"I demand tests." Dave was shocked.

"You can have all the tests you like, Dave, but you are not Julie's father."

"You lied to me. Deceived me all these years."

"Get over it. I had to—many times."

"Does he know?" Julie asked her mother.

"Marco. No, I never told him. Never saw him again. I should have told you though, Julie."

"Mum, it's okay. I can marry Harry now. I'm so happy."

"Happy," Dave shouted. "What about me? I've just been told I'm not your father. I'm in shock. Not to mention I have another son I knew nothing about."

"You'll always be my dad," Julie hugged Dave.

Her sudden change of heart was quite startling, but at least she didn't hate me anymore, Dave thought to himself.

"I shouldn't be pleased about all this—and yes, I am shocked—but I love Harry. It's all rather messy, I realise that, but Harry said Wilf was his father and always will be in every way except biologically and I feel the same about you, Dad, I suppose—or I will do once I get used to the idea. I can't wait to tell Harry the good news."

She kissed them both and hurried from the house.

Six months later

"He's not coming then?" Harry asked, as they posed for yet more photographs.

"No, he's not. Since they decided to divorce, they've hardly spoken and now Dad works at the New York office, he's near to the twins, so he'll be okay. He's already got a new girlfriend. He sends his good wishes."

"He's been very generous financially. We'll go over and visit when things settle down," Harry smiled.

"Mmm. Maybe visit Corfu as well," Julie laughed.

"Why not," Harry answered. "Look, Mum's in tears again. Always cries at weddings."

"I'm glad you've forgiven her."

"Of course I have. We all make mistakes, and if Dad can forgive her, then I certainly shouldn't have a problem. They're great together, always have been."

"My brothers have said I'll always be their little sister. It was such a relief, although it still feels strange to think they're your half-brothers as well. We must promise never to keep secrets, Harry."

"I promise," he whispered.

"So do I," Julie replied.

THE CHILD

KATH CROFT

The child snuggled up to me, so close as if to climb inside me. I smiled down at her, wondering what it was that had made her choose to sit beside me. Her pink tulle dress spread around her like a gossamer web, as she wrapped her smooth plump arms around my waist. The noise of the party was strident and I had to bend my head down close to her mouth to hear her whisper, 'I have a secret!'

'Have you, sweetheart?' My heart froze, in fear of what she might tell me. How would I deal with such a terrible secret? I had dreaded hearing those words all my adult life; they constantly haunted my subconscious mind. Fear and panic rose within me like gall and I could feel the vomit rising in the back of my throat. I knew I had to remain calm and allow her to speak to tell me her worst fear. She had after all, chosen me, and who better than me to understand her secret? And how was I to deal with it after she had told the horror she had suffered? Did I find her mother and tell her what had been happening to her precious, beautiful child on this, her own wonderful wedding day? No, I couldn't do that, besides I didn't yet know the perpetrator of this terrible tragedy, unfolding here. And what if the perpetrator was the bridegroom, this child's new Daddy? It had happened before and, in all probability, would happen again many times. Wasn't that a truth I already knew for myself? Perhaps I should call the police. I pulled her close to me and whispered, 'You can tell me.' She nodded her head in serious concentration. Her hair was sprinkled with tiny beads of glitter, shining like the clear sparkle of her eyes.

'Is it a nice secret or a not so nice secret?'

'I don't know.' She shrugged her thin little body in confusion at my question. 'What's a nasty secret?'

'Well, it's usually something that makes you unhappy. Are you unhappy about your secret?'

'Oh yes,' she replied. 'I think so. My mummy is going to have a baby, but I haven't to tell anyone yet, because my new daddy doesn't know yet and he might be cross, so it's Mummy's and my secret for now.'

She smiled serenely at me and said, 'you won't tell, will you?'

'No, sweetheart, I won't tell.'

The ice in my belly melted and my heart began to return to its normal rhythm. I felt relieved and drained of emotion in one huge sense of suppressed anxiety. Yet again, my own secret remained untold!

THE GEEK'S DEN

NICK STEAD

A chair scraped across the floor and Siobhan looked up. This promised to be the most interesting thing that happened all lesson.

Mrs Jones led Chris Sergeant out of the room. The teacher kept her voice low but it still carried through the door, muffled only slightly. Nosy classmates listened in.

Marissa scoffed at what she heard. "Is Mrs Jones blind? There's no secret what's up with her. Either she's a lesbo or a tranny. Why else would she get all mardy at her full name?"

"Yeah," Siobhan agreed. "Bet her house is full of lesbo porn and shit."

Jade gave a wicked grin. "I'll give you a fiver if you can get pictures."

"Easy money," Siobhan answered.

But it wasn't.

First she took to following Chris around, though the stupid bitch never went anywhere exciting – no after school meetings with forbidden lovers or anything like that. School finished, Chris went home and she retreated to her room. So boring.

Next Siobhan tried knocking on the door of the house and posing as a friend. It worked – Mrs Sergeant invited her in. Chris was too shocked to say anything and Siobhan got to see the inside of her room. But while it was filled with boyish things, there was nothing damning to take back to Jade.

So she continued acting like Chris's friend. It was as tedious as their school work but it was no longer about the money. If she returned to her real friends empty-handed they might take to ridiculing her.

"You don't have to suffer alone, you know," she said one day, back in the geek's den. She reached out to grasp the other girl's hand, oozing false friendship. "It's nothing to be ashamed of. You can tell me how you really feel, I won't laugh."

Chris shied away, horrified. Damn it, she'd pushed too far. But then Chris surprised her. "You promise you won't tell?"

"Cross my heart."

"Okay." They went into the basement and through to a hidden door. "Even Mum doesn't know about this."

A sex dungeon? Siobhan's stomach fluttered with excitement, her phone in hand. This promised to be way better than a stash of porn.

The stench hit her the moment Chris opened the door. She gagged and reeled backwards, but Chris seemed unaffected. Siobhan pinched her nose and followed inside.

It was pitch black. Siobhan used her phone as a torch, the light bringing only disappointment at first, the room seemingly empty. Then the beam found a pair of eyes. They stared sightlessly up at her out of a mangled face, teeth grinning between strips of torn flesh. Siobhan screamed.

"I didn't want to," Chris said. "But he told me it was either my neighbours or my family."

Siobhan turned to run but there was something monstrous blocking the doorway now, dark and malevolent.

"I'm sorry," Chris whispered in her ear. Pain erupted in her lower back, one, two, three times. Blood gushed as the blade withdrew. And Siobhan fell.

THE SECRET TRAVELLER

SARA BURGESS

He packs a few belongings in a small bag with a little food. There is a plastic bottle of water with a long straw that fits through the lid. The airport excites him, the plane on which he will travel roams up and down the runway like a nervous dog. Its turbines thrill him as they whine. He watches the people lining up, ascending the gangway into the fuselage. They remind him of little dolls he had when he was a boy. He fixed them into their seats and flew the plane round their kitchen, annoying his mother till she shooed him out with the brush. She is dead now. What does he have left but a new life over the sea?

Fixing himself into his place on the plane, he takes his chance. His ear defenders vibrate, such is the roar as the plane jolts out of its taxiing and points upward. It thrusts at an obscene angle and rushes into the clouds at a pace. He feels his skin stick to his face, his eyelids peel back and his fingers claw at the wind. He has no breath and already he is a limpet, stuck to the undercarriage of the great machine. Tiny droplets of ice form in his pores like a coating of marcasite and he is gone.

His body surges forward, at one with the body of this gigantic metal bird glinting in the sun, for some nine hours, preserved from decay by ice. Its legitimate passengers are oblivious, their thoughts filled with their own small lives. One even smaller is snuffed out beneath their baggage, as a drop in altitude with Heathrow beckoning, effects a rapid thaw on it.

At a certain height he peels off and tumbles into the cool blue air over a patchwork mish-mash of gardens in Clapham. How many look up to the skies upon hearing the hopeful sound of an airliner approaching its destination, to note with surprise this speck hurtling from its base? The impending impact strikes horror into the heart of any bystander as gravity exerts its influence.

His remains are a missile set to cause mayhem, threading darkly towards the earth. A crash, a whump, a crater in a garden only yards from a leisurely chap enjoying a snooze on a sun lounger at the back of his house. What outrage at the laxity of airports in foreign climes, the carnage he could have caused, never mind the devastation to his own sad body, caused by unimaginable desperation.

What life can be so bad to willingly engage in such a death?

LOCATIONS - 2019

EXTERNAL ADJUDICATOR'S COMPETITION

BABYLON

GARETH CLEGG

The usual dusty trail died on the approach to New Babylon, giving way to unprecedented greenery around the rich loamy fields. I'd heard about the fabled fertile earth surrounding the city, but seeing it for myself was a totally different matter. Huge stalks of corn reached for the blue skies, bright yellow kernels reflecting the brilliant morning sun.

Hell, even the temperature seemed more natural. No more sweat dripping from the burning wastes I was used to travelling. I pulled my loose duster tighter about me as a shiver ran down into the small of my aching back. I patted my grey mare as she shied sideways, spooked by something. My hand dropped to my side, unclipping the leather strap on my holster that secured my revolver. I scanned the ground for snakes but nothing slithered through the lush grass at the side of the road. But with the height it had grown to, who knew? I was mighty impressed with the approach, and if this was just the outskirts, I couldn't imagine my response to the hanging gardens.

Folks tending the fields waved and called welcome as I

passed. I tipped my hat in response, and the fenced road soon became an avenue lined by huge trees. The gentle breeze brushed the bright leaves, whispering its song as small critters scurried up the branches, leaping across the approach road where the tree limbs reached over, grasping for their comrades on the opposite side. With all the sights of nature in its prime, I hadn't even noticed the roadway. I glanced back over my shoulder seeing where it emerged from the desert trail through the badland, straight as a cliff edge.

Dappled light danced over the fine stonework, shadows swaying over the perfectly sized grey rectangles as the mare's hooves clacked out a slow and steady rhythm.

The outline of the city rose like dark mist forming huge walls and turrets. The hanging gardens split the stone walls, climbing like poison ivy. Thick limbs extended away from the wall, growing towards the lush vegetation outside the city. And there, swaying in the light breeze they hung— bodies. Thousands of them, the sickly sweet smell already seeping into me, like death.

The base of the great walled city wasn't paved, who in their right mind would want to go walking below the liquid seeping from those hanging above? The bodies of those condemned to a tortuous death came in two varieties, the ones hanging by the neck - their dark bloated bodies the first to rot, and then there were the others, condemned to a slow demise.

They hung in metal cages, their tortured souls condemned to starve with no food or water. They seldom lasted more than a few days, but it was an eternity of torture compared to the swift drop and a broken neck.

But this was Babylon. And they didn't suffer from crimes within the city, mainly because of the Draconian law enforcement. Every convicted criminal had only two outcomes: tree or cage.

It might seem brutal to some. How could death be the outcome for every crime? Surely murder wasn't equivalent to stealing a loaf of bread. But this was how they did things here, and people knew it. Posters plastered over the walls on the approach reminded visitors of what lawbreakers could expect. No exceptions, no claims of ignorance, no deviation - the law was absolute, and that's why it was a utopia for those that wanted to live in harmony with their fellows.

The grey mare skittered sideways as a particularly unpleasant waft of foetid warm air blew across the huge entrance. The sickly sweet rot, a constant smell in the background, suddenly dialled up to fucking unpleasant. I coughed and dug my knees in tight, directing the beast back into line.

The gate guards continued with their business, seemingly unperturbed. How the hell did they put up with this all day? I was already feeling the urge to retch.

Grasping my inner core of willpower, I bit back the bilious taste in my throat and tried breathing through my mouth. It helped, a little.

A rider in the group ahead coughed and unleashed a stream of warm chunks onto the cobbles, splattering around a guard's pristine boot.

So, these were the Hanging Gardens of Babylon - one of the seven wonders of our accursed world.

BURIED TREASURE

SOPHIE ALDERHEART

Buried in distant sands,
A shell of pearlescent blue in a box of English oak,
A moment of innocence preserved in the cliff's shadow.

Ocean waves rumble,
Thundering turquoise and bubbling foam echo for miles,
Cresting the beaches of the Portuguese coast.

Even through the whispering nights,
It pursues the land in its swirling dance,
Unable to touch upon its buried charge.

Sizzling sun bakes the white gold sands,
Shards of diamond light inviting and pure,
Guarding the shadows with its glamorous mirage.

Oh home of golden shores
Sun that ever shines and sea that ever watches
Protect that shell, that piece of childhood love
Till I return for it once more.

CASTLE HILL

SUSIE FIELD

Looking down from Castle Hill
A beautiful world, perfect and still.
The setting sun its crimson glow
Casting shadows on the earth below.
So many memories slowly unfold
Kept close in my heart - stories untold.

EXODUS

VIVIEN TEASDALE

Object: mirror

We left early, sun bronzing the hedges
and the mist clinging
to the black sods, newly ploughed.

We stared as familiar houses
slid past, faster and faster. The truck
growled menacingly, then subsided
into a grumbling purr under the driver's hand.

We knew the morning songs, the country scents,
picked out the flowers, saw the trees we'd climbed,
the fields tramped, the walls we'd clambered over.

A few folk were stooking the wheat,
shrinking in the wing mirror, our lives torn apart.
Ahead was an alien place, thronging
with noise and confusion.

We smelled noxious fumes, the unknown,
and shrank back against cold indifferent leather,
unable to see where we had come from.

FORTY-NINE

GARETH CLEGG

Forty-nine, again!

Katsumi gathered the yarrow sticks, sorting them into neat piles, and placed them back in their protective case. It was the third identical reading of the I Ching and it didn't bode well. It couldn't be chance, it was a foretelling of grave danger. Four represented death and nine equated to pain, suffering and torture. So forty-nine was the worst combination of the two - a painful death.

Was it hers? She gripped her ancient peachwood amulet tight in both hands, a final gift from her mother on her deathbed, then placed it back around her neck. The carved Komainu lion-dog hung warm against her skin, reassuring, protecting, but she would need to speak to the master on his return in the morning.

A shiver ran down the young girl's spine as rain continued its deluge on the wooden roof. It was more like someone pouring a bucketful of metal balls from a pachinko machine. The wind joined the fray, a tormented beast howling, tearing at the shutters of the old temple.

A huge slam resounded as the storm forced one shutter

open, flapping wildly in the tumult. Katsumi rose, walking calmly to the opening. Her white silk kimono flowed about her as if swirling in unseen underwater currents. Bright red lips pursed as she approached the whistling gale pouring into the shrine. Bells hummed as they shook and paper charms fluttered on the dark wooden posts supporting the roof, but didn't break free.

The tatami mats crunched underfoot, Katsumi scrunching them with her bare feet - as she'd done since being a child. The course texture of the traditional flooring was reassuring. Icy spray blasted her pristine coal-black hair, the water beading on her straight locks and dripping to her shoulders. As if she hadn't been cold enough, now she was soaked too. As she reached for the wooden frame, it slammed again, four times in rapid succession. She pulled her hand back with a gasp. Something was trying to make itself heard.

Lightning flashed, lighting up the red torii arch outside. Its shadow leapt into the room for an instant before slithering off into the dark corners. Lanterns suspended from the wooden beams swayed, spreading eerie shadows around the place, and black shapes ebbed and flowed like tidal waters on a much faster schedule.

"Enough," Katsumi cried, flinging her pale arms wide. "Spirits of air and fire, guardians of this temple, reveal that which does not belong here and cast it out. Begone darkness, flee before the holy light and protective spirits of this ancient site."

A shriek erupted, echoing around the room, followed by splintering gouges in the walls as great claws glowed with a soft red outline as she thrust it out.

The shutter slammed for a final time, and Katsumi dropped to her knees, sweat beading on her forehead, her breathing ragged. Though the storm still raged outside, the dread melted from the pit of her stomach, and she drew a deep breath. In through her nose then she held it, forcing it down to her centre, before slowly releasing it through her painted lips.

"Thank you, spirits," she whispered to the not so empty room. Motes twinkled, like stars in the night sky, as they returned to their resting places, fading into the beams, the matted floor, the bells and the wooden walls. Only the air kami remained suspended above her in the rafters, but they too melted away, distant dying suns, until all was silent and calm descended to fill her.

Katsumi stared as a vertical slit of light burst forth before her. Shielding her eyes, she waited for it to fade enough to see the doorway. All around the temple interior faded to a translucent glow that hugged the plain room where she sat cross-legged in the centre.

"That was good, Katsumi," the old man called as he walked towards her. Master Asahina stepped spritely for a priest of his years, crossing the distance with little need for the gnarled wooden stick he carried to aid him. He reached, gripping her outstretched hand and pulled her to her feet. "You did well." His voice, though friendly, contained a hint of something withheld.

"Is there something further you wish to say, master?"

His grizzled features scrunched, deep ravines appearing around his mouth, but he remained silent. Regardless, his eyes spoke volumes, catching Katsumi with a telltale widening, something he did when not wanting to speak within earshot of others. She lowered her gaze to the ground, modern flooring showing through the holographic tatami matting. "Apologies, Master. My thanks for your generous praise, though I do not believe I am deserving of it."

"Why do you say that?"

She glanced to him, teeth nipping at her top lip. "My actions could have been swifter. I allowed an entity to invade the sacred halls. I should have recognised it earlier and prevented its entrance while sealing the shutters."

Asahina looked up at her petite frame as he stroked his wispy beard. With his back bent as it was, he stood almost a foot shorter than her. "You need to appreciate your success more, and failings less. We will talk of this later, at the temple."

"Yes, Master."

The trip across town only took an hour, but the bustle of people on public transport made her anxious. Katsumi's stomach clenched, and a dribble of icy sweat dripped down her back. She dealt with entities and spiritual manifestations, so why couldn't she deal with the press of humanity all around?

The mass transit system roared away from the silver towers of glowing neon in the centre that clawed at the sparkling dome of energy encasing the city. Spots of light flickered in the pale blue as the roiling dark clouds pounded at the exterior, searching for a weak spot to force their way inside.

The sensation of speed was lost in the carriage's comfort, but the closer they got to the shield wall, the fewer people remained. Many of them left at the last suburbs of Nakano and Shinjuku. Beyond, there was nothing of use to the city folk of New Tokyo. A few still visited the old shrine in Suginami, but they were rare. Some relied on virtual representations, elaborate holo-projections, much as she'd trained in. Most immersed themselves in full digital constructs, offering their prayers and gifts to their ancestors online. Technology was the god of New Tokyo now.

She led the way onto the platform, still wearing the white kimono. She adhered to the ritual dress-code regardless of the stares and whispers of the public. Hers was a solitary existence, nothing to disrupt her thoughts, self-contemplation and learning. Her days were filled with reading from ancient tomes and teachings from the old man himself.

The trip to the holo-projection suite was a welcome change. Tech abounded within the city and in the hands of every citizen. Though the priest called it an emotional crutch, the idea of personal implants seemed astonishing in her eyes. She'd love to try it, if only for a few moments. Devices built into the user's body, the ability to communicate with anyone connected to the network with but a thought. It was almost like magic. But she knew better than to focus on fanciful dreams, having devoted her life to the spirits.

They travelled in silence until passing under the great torii archway. Its vibrant red clashed with the natural greenery and tranquillity surrounding the shrine. Katsumi tore her eyes from the ancient wooden monument. "Master, I felt you wished to say more earlier?"

He grumbled something under his breath before saying, "Yes, but with too many others around, it was not the time to do so."

Katsumi waited, she'd learned patience would best net

her the answers she sought, but the old priest remained preoccupied. "And now?" she prompted as they approached the magnificent Shinto shrine.

"Hmm. Tea, then talking." He continued grumbling as he passed her, entering the building first as was his way.

Katsumi held back, closing her eyes and opening her soul to the millions of kami following her every move. She saw them as she had in the simulation, twinkling pinpricks of light in the ground and rocks at her feet. They swam through the water, cascading into flowing streams beneath the wooden bridge, or danced through burning flames within paper lanterns. Above her, air kami flitted in the gentle breeze or floated down to torment their earthbound kin before leaping back into the sky. She imagined the tinkling laughter from the flighty spirits and the grumbles from the others at their frivolity.

"Come on, girl. This tea won't make itself now, will it?"

She picked up her pace, shuffling steps taking her into the shrine as fast as she was able. It seemed an apprentice's work was never done, but a gleaming smile grew across her pale features, glad to be home again.

HUDDERSFIELD ROYAL INFIRMARY
SUSIE FIELD

I'm Colin the computer and I work in A&E
No one even knows my name and no one speaks to me.
I'm very stressed and overworked, I rarely take a break
I sit in line and don't complain - it's hard for goodness' sake.
They bang my keys and spin me round, they simply do
not care
Sometimes they gather in little groups, just simply stand
and stare.
I always seem to get the blame when things are not quite
right
But I only store what they give to me—morning, noon and
night.
An X-ray here, another scan and even a ruptured spleen
Dashing about, here and there, switching from screen to
screen.
Zooming in and zooming out, please make up your mind
Something else they must have lost or simply cannot find.

Poor Carol's in reception and she doesn't like that crowd.
It's busier than ever and they're noisy, rude and loud.

Carl has done much better, he's sitting with a nurse
A private little office, now that must be a first.
Not a major accident or another late-night fight
I clearly heard the sirens and saw a bright blue light.
They all descend on Carol who's always first in line
I think I'll take a breather, whilst I've still got a little time.
Fat chance of that 'cos they're heading my way
Coffee cups balanced on a wobbly tray.
Oh no, she's tripped and I've swallowed the lot
My insides are melting and it's burning hot.
I splutter and spark with all my lights flashing
They cannot believe I'm actually crashing.
Their faces contort with absolute horror
Now I know they will miss me come tomorrow.

They're wheeling in Carl to take my place
Oh, the expression on his smug little face.
He cannot believe he'll now have to work
All those duties so far he's managed to shirk.
Darkness descends and I'm all alone
In a dusty old store room without a phone.
I can hear distant voices and lots of chatter
Everyone's having a good old natter.
I wish I was back there in A and E
I know it was busy but it suited me.

RUNNING MAN

KATH CROFT

He runs. The blackness as solid as the rock entombing him makes his footfall hard to predict. The electric lights dim the further he runs from the other men. They remain, huddled together, giving comfort, one to the other. So deep are they within this vast tomb, that the heat increases as the atmosphere becomes fetid, the un-replenished air slowly souring. His anxiety increases as the others talk of escape, willing those above them to move the fallen roof. He can hear the others calling him back above the incessant drone in his ears; he runs further into the blackness. Up a level and beyond the dim light of the last electric lamps, the light from his helmet giving a candle's faint glow to show the ground as each step hits the uneven surface. On and up, the ground rising slowly in a constant curve until the fall halts his progress. Here there is no light, only the dull glow from his helmet's lamp. His fear of the lamp dimming to nothing turns him back, and now the downward curve returns him to sit at the edge of the group of men. They chatter like the incessant nattering of wives in the market, those same women, who have lit candles and left them to glow in their house windows, before they run, demented to the pithead. Now they are silent, waiting, somewhere above the men's heads, each wanting, needing news, any news to ease this torment.

The drone increases, louder, dominant and insistent. Fearing the unstable ground will again collapse, he holds his head, trying to block out the sounds -humour; so full of false bravery, his ears deny all the remaining sounds of life. The other men are rejoicing in their contact with the world above them; a world he fears he will never rejoin. They all, each one in turn, now speak of their hopes for their children's future, favourite food they will eat, what they will say to those, up there, waiting, but he, unable to hope, speaks harshly to the voice he so loves, so sure he will never hold her or touch her beloved face again

The droning shatters the solid rock and a voice shouts out their names as a face, new to this closeted world, emerges from the solid rock. Fresh air and warm food, and now all but he believe they will soon be safe. This new face now gives the orders and the strongest of the miners, the one who chivvied them into believing they would be saved, must take his turn with the others to enter the capsule. This saviour, their hero, must be the last to leave this hellhole, and he wonders at the courage of this man from another land, another world, who gives up his freedom to save their souls.

The capsule is, their arms clamped beside their bodies, as if they are in deaths rigor. Slowly, one by one in the darkness of night, they emerge, heroes returning and the world embraces them. But he sees only a coffin, and his dread on entering its darkness fills him with hysteria; he needs to run, to run out his fear; fear of this solid blackness,

blackness as solid as the rock entombing his mind and now encasing his body!

But in this new freedom, a freedom his mind cannot accept, he can only run, step after painful step.breath. He stops. Hands behind his legs, his forehead kissing his knees, he gulps in the cool night air. He raises his face to the heaven's darkness and sees a new darkness, sparkling with candle points of light. With his hands over his ears, he tries to shut out the drilling silent sound of blackness. Looking at each point of light, absorbing them, feeling their truth, he turns around and around until he can turn no more and falls to the ground, beating his hands on the desert's rough surface and he screams.

Again candle-lit room and to the voice he so loves; she holds him to her and he buries his head into the softness of her body and cries. Finally, he sleeps.

SEAHOUSES

OWEN TOWNEND

On benches facing ocean,
Gran and I watched out
from the top of a slope.

Setting down my rucksack,
I felt around but
my umbrella was gone.

Clearing her throat, Grandma
popped my brolly
with a sly little smirk.

"I wanted to show how easy it is to steal this."

I took it back
as the RNLI ran down
from the pub
to the docks.

As Gran watched them
I thought about Hell,
high water
and her smile.

THE ABBEY

SUSIE FIELD

I cannot sleep, yet I'm so tired. Maybe it's the excitement of this weekend break. The first break I've taken alone and it's much better than I expected. Today I explored the twisting cobbled streets leading to Whitby Abbey and then had lunch at the Angel Hotel, which is now a Wetherspoons so that at least felt familiar. I'm looking forward to visiting the Abbey tomorrow and St Mary's Church nestling on the cliff top. Why wait until tomorrow? I'm wide awake and although it's 2am, I'm restless.

I slip my warm coat over my pyjamas and lace up my sturdy walking boots. The corridor outside my room is quiet so I carefully close the door, not wanting to wake my fellow guests. I use the stairs instead of the lift and feel relieved reception is unmanned, though I can hear voices. Slipping through the main doors I breathe in the cold clean air as I stand beneath the whale bones to admire the view. The night is still and clear, a mist shrouding the church and Abbey in the distance.

I turn to the right and take the quickest route into the

town. The streets are deserted but I'm not afraid. Maybe apprehensive but also excited although I cannot explain why I should feel this way. The Angel Pub is silent and I sit awhile at one of the outside tables watching the sea creep into the harbour. After crossing the swing bridge, I notice a group of youths in a nearby doorway. They glance in my direction but thankfully turn away engrossed in their own world.

It's dropping cold, and a stiff wind whips my hair around my face. I pull my hood tighter as I continue my way through the dark, cobbled streets until I reach the Abbey steps. I can hear the sea crashing against the shore, the waves suddenly fierce and threatening as I steadily climb the 199 steps. The mist hangs heavy in the air and I shiver beneath my heavy coat wishing I'd worn a sweater over my pyjamas. Heading towards St Mary's Church, I ask myself why I am making this journey alone in the middle of the night but I have no answer. The church door is locked and I silently curse as I pull my mobile from my coat pocket. I keep my head down as I follow the beam of light on the path leading to the back of the church and through the graveyard. The Abbey stares down menacingly as if watching my every move. I cannot enter, the gates are locked and bolted. Heading towards the cliff top, I stop and rest on one of the memorial benches. It's so tranquil and beautiful, and I sit awhile enjoying the ambience of this beautiful place. Gazing up at the stars, I close my eyes for a moment, lost in their tranquillity.

Suddenly sensing someone watching me, I slowly turn but I'm alone in the darkness, yet the feeling lingers. Something brushes against my cheek and I shiver as the wind once more whips away my hood. A hand reaches towards me, caressing my face and hair. I'm lost in the sensuous embrace and close my eyes savouring the touch as it fills my mind and body with an unfamiliar longing. I cannot understand what is happening as these strange sensations threaten to consume me - then it's suddenly over. I glance around and yet I'm still alone.

Struggling to my feet I hurry back towards the Abbey steps stretching endlessly before me. The youths are still in the doorway by the swing bridge and they turn once more in my direction, their faces void of all expression, their eyes glazed and vacant. They move towards me but I start to run. They give chase but soon tire and fall breathlessly onto the hard stone cobbles. My sudden strength and energy know no bounds. My feet barely touch the ground, as if I'm flying through the air and it feels wonderful.

When I reach my hotel, I feel excited and alive, ignoring the stares of the night security guard as he looks at me questioningly. Hurrying to my room, I stop for a moment by the window to stare at the Abbey in the distance. It stares back. Closing the curtains, I pull off my boots and coat and fall into bed exhausted by my adventure.

I wake to the morning sunshine streaming through the crack in the curtains. I pull them back with a flourish but the sun's blinding me, sapping my strength. I can see the Abbey in the distance and remember the dream, still so vivid in my mind. As I turn, I notice my boots lying on the floor, muddy and wet. My coat is thrown on the chair next to the bed. The pillow is stained red with blood - fresh and wet to the touch. With trembling fingers, I reach for the wounds on my neck. What are they? What has happened to me? The blood drips steadily onto my pyjama top as I rush into the bathroom rinsing my face, desperately trying to wipe away the sticky substance oozing from my neck into the wash basin. My heart is beating so fast as I raise my head towards the small mirror on the wall, dreading what I might see - but there is nothing. I am no more.

THE CORPSE WAY

VIVIEN TEASDALE

Object: Brooch

'No, Tilly. See what it's like out there!' Leonard grabbed my shoulder and dragged me to the door. Flinging it open, he pushed me outside. The wind tried to push me back into the dubious warmth of the farmhouse kitchen, but Leonard was having none of it. Holding me in a firm grasp, he forced me to confront the gale, which responded by lashing icy fingers across my cheeks, wrenching my hair loose, and wrapping it tightly round my neck, half choking me.

'It won't always be like this,' I gasped. 'Surely the wind is dying a little.'

'Aye, but it springs to life just as easily. Think on, lass. We're sheltered in the valley. What d'you think it'll be like up on't Scar, eh? You've never been up there when the sky's raven black, rain soaking every stitch on you an' it's cold as death.'

'Leonard! Think on yourself, man.' His wife pushed him out of the way and brought me back inside. 'Come on, love. It's not your place ...'

I twisted myself free. 'That's just it, Mistress Avice. It *is* my place. There's no-one else. My father must be accompanied by family.' I turned to Leonard. 'I will go! If I have to straggle behind, shunned by you all, I'll follow. I will see my father safe to his last resting place.'

'Then it's time we started.' Edith, Leonard's sister, thrust open the door, letting in the freezing air. Like me, she was dressed in boots, heavy skirt and even heavier cape. 'The girl is right, but she needs better company than your rough lads.'

Edith didn't wait for argument, simply turned and strode back into the yard, to the men, standing and shuffling on feet that were already cold. 'Take up the burden,' she instructed them. For a second, they looked at Leonard, watching from the doorway. He shrugged, then nodded. Four moved into place, bending in unison to grasp the handles of the wicker coffin. Two men walked ahead, two men walked behind. Edith and I followed, ignored by them all.

Villagers lined the route, crossing themselves as the coffin passed, saying a short prayer for the man they had worked with for so many years. They watched as the cortège set off along the path down the valley. Above, the sky still grumbled, throwing gusts of wind at the walkers.

The way led the pallbearers through meadows, over East Gill beck and up a rough track which kept us just under the brow of the hill, giving slight shelter from the north wind. The teams stopped at each coffin stone, resting the wicker basket there while the men stamped their frozen feet and shook life into icy hands. Then the new team swung up their load and plodded on along grey scree tracks, tripping and skidding on the loose stones, or down through woods, still bare with no sign of Spring.

Not once did they look back at us. We trudged silently behind until, as we arrived at Ivelet Bridge, Edith stumbled and fell, screaming in pain as her shoulder hit the sharp rocks nearby.

'What now!' Leonard snapped, as if we'd had been pestering them all morning. The coffin was, once again, set down. Turning back, the men helped Edith to her feet.

'Don't worry about me,' she said, rubbing her shoulder. 'There's a hard pull up Gunnerside yet. Keep moving.'

The men shrugged, retracing their steps to where the coffin lay. We were a subdued party that struggled up the fell side, kicking over peaty clumps as we searched for the winding, little used path. Collars were now turned up, uselessly, against the drizzle that turned to rain and finally to sleet before we toiled into Blades and a night's rest. Tomorrow was for the final miles down into Grinton.

'You came, then.' The old lady stumbled forward. 'I wasn't sure ... Oh, girl, it's good to see you.' I just managed to catch my grandmother as she staggered. The old woman was thin, fevered, and the villagers kept their distance, though the two groups walked alongside each other, escorting the body across Grinton bridge to the lychgate of St Andrew's where the vicar waited to lead us to the graveside and my brief goodbye to my father.

. . .

'I'm sorry, there's no place for you here, girl.' Grandmother squeezed my hand as we lay, huddled together under the grubby blanket of her bed, but she stuck to her earlier decision. 'Master Caygill has offered to keep you. His wife needs a companion. It's a good position. You'll want for nothing.'

I turned away. Grandmother was right, of course, but I knew there was more to Master Caygill's offer than consideration for his wife. 'I could stay for a while, Gran. You look pale. I could take ...'

Gran shook her head. 'No. You leave, tomorrow, with the others.' She gasped, beginning to retch. Clutching a rag to her mouth, she doubled up in pain, staining the cloth with gobs of blood. I ran to fetch water. Gran accepted it, easing her throat for a while, but kept her shawl pulled tightly around and over her head, hiding the growing sores on her neck.

'Go, Tilly. Be a good girl. Work hard,' Gran wheezed, resting her hand on my head for a moment as I stood beside the bed the next morning. 'It will be the last time we meet on this earth. Take this.' The old woman took a ribbon from around her neck, looping it over my head. Strung from the ribbon was a small, pewter brooch in the shape of a cross, the pin bent and misshapen. 'It has protected me through the years, please God it will protect you.'

Choking back my tears, I embraced the old woman, feeling bones through lumpy flesh under the woollen shawl.

'Goodbye, Gran,' I whispered, kissing her once more as Edith appeared at the doorway.

'Come on, lass,' she said, then she too hugged the old woman. They both knew I would need all the support I could find from now on.

'Take my blessing with you, girl.' Gran cried as I joined Edith and the Keld men for the walk back to our village.

We had come to bury the dead. None of us had yet realised that death was now walking with us as we returned home beneath the blackening sky.

THE DARKEST PLACE IN THE WORLD

SARA BURGESS

Bella remembers in the dark. Her memories are stored like letters in a scratched and dusty bureau. She picks one out, the book she used to read to Joe. It is large, like a dinner tray, on her lap. The cover is glossy, the pages printed on good paper, thick between her finger and thumb. She closes her eyes and recalls how it feels to turn each sumptuous page, imagines the sound of her voice saying the words while Joe wriggles under the sheet beside her. The dark here is like inky water seeping into your skin, but she knows the story by heart and draws the title in the close air in front of her: *the old, dark house.*

She knows every picture as they have studied it together many times, their tousled heads bowed, and Joe's spidery hand crawling across the page. His thin, white fingers point first at the crooked chimney, then follow the silvery web down the wall, leap to the black cat's back, arched like a clumsy aitch, then tiptoe towards the light that peeps through the open door. In her mind he says it again, 'read it, Mummy,' and she does. *Deep in the old, dark forest there is an old, dark house. It is so hard to find that most people have forgotten it is there.*

The bureau is the only thing that keeps her sane in this cold, grey room, as she lies on the hard bed frame trying to shut out the sounds that seep through the stone walls like sea mist. The bureau is stuffed. She has made it so. Brim full of happy times that she uses to blot out the bad thoughts that sneak in like starving alley cats. The moments of rippling laughter, the sun shining on a golden beach as the blue waves curl over the sand with a flash of frothy foam, the wind shaking a branch full of leaves or whipping your hair into a knot, the taste of creamy vanilla, the tinkling aria from a distant ice cream van, the explosive crimson fountain as the blade plunges...

No, stop. Stop now. Birdsong, starlight, fizzy lemonade, angels singing, la la la, la la la...

'Jesus, Bella, will you freakin' shut up?'

'La la la...'

'Bella, shut your freakin' MOUTH.'

There is a searing pain in her cheek followed by the dull thud as her head bashes against the wall, then black, smoky darkness.

'This started before Joe was born.'

The lady doctor with the twinkly blue eyes behind half-moon glasses, and crinkly red hair that looks like a child's scribble says '*mmm, and...*'

Bella watches, fascinated, as her bony hands appear from the tangle of brightly-coloured knitted robe draped around her body. The flash of a gold pen scratches on her tiny notebook. It reminds Bella of something, the quick memories rushing up like hot, yellow bile. She starts speaking before it gets to her throat.

'When Dan and me first got together...' Bella knows what this is. She has seen enough prison dramas where the psychiatrist lets the patient talk it all out. But this isn't scripted. The finish isn't written neatly at the end of a pile of papers. If she wants to get out of here, she has to fight. But does that mean telling the truth, or telling them what they want to hear?

'When Dan and me first got together, I never thought we would start a family. He was exciting. And sexy. It was like being on a fairground ride, whizzing around everywhere, loud music in your ears, racy clubs, fast cars. I didn't know at the time...that they weren't *his* fast cars, and it wasn't really his money at the clubs. But when I found out, I was already pregnant.'

Bella waits for the *mmm* but it doesn't come, just the pen scratching, a page flipped over, the shrink shifting her bum round in the chair. She feels a bubble start to rise but carries on, quashing it.

'It just got worse from that moment on. The first thing he did was accuse me of going with someone else. I couldn't believe it. I would never do that. I didn't realise it at the time but he was talking about himself. That's what he was doing. That's what he had always been doing. I was just one of a long line of... slappers... in his mind. But I was the stupid one who went and got pregnant.' She waits again for some kind of human reaction, but there is none. It is like talking to one of the cold brick walls in her room.

'By the time Joe was due I never knew from one day to the next whether I would see him. I was still stupid enough to think that Dan would change when his son was born. More fool me.' Bella feels the bubble start to rise again as she notices the noughts and crosses at the end of the fine tip of the gold pen. Her voice steps up a note.

'So when I gave birth to a crocodile and the midwife chopped off his tail, I decided to join a nunnery.'

Dr Jones' pale blue eyes flick up like opening shutters. She holds Bella's furious stare.

'It's not a good idea to try to manipulate me, Bella. Your last comment tells me more about you than anything else you have said. It's pure Freud. Religious repression, guilt, castration complex, deferred violence to the male... it's why you're here in a nutshell, so why don't we get down to the real conversation, huh?'

Bella holds on to the chair to stop herself flipping over.

'I'm here to move the situation on.' Dr Jones says the first six words with her eyes closed and her mousy eyebrows like tiny bridges. 'What we come up with here affects your future. Take my advice. Stop screwing about.'

'Deep in the old, dark forest there is an old, dark house. It is so hard to find that most people have forgotten it is there. Once there was a fine path which led to its wrought iron gates, through a beautiful garden with roses and fruit trees all the way up to the magnificent front door with a big brass knocker. But over the years the forest grew and grew, and brambles, ferns and grasses grew over the path, ivy covered the walls and all the people simply forgot that the house was ever there.'

'That's good, Bell', carry on.'

'Once it belonged to a very grand family. They were so rich they wore French velvet and Italian lace every day. They were so rich they could eat banoffee pie for breakfast and sardines for supper...'

'That's disgusting. Hey, Bell' I'm sorry, you know.' Bella sits up sharply, the hard bedframe creaks, she peers through her hair at her roommate.

'I thought you wanted to listen to this,' she says in a grey voice.

'I do, go on. It's just...I'm sorry, you know...for hitting you like that.'

'Yeah, well...' Bella tries to speak but a lump sticks in her throat.

'It's just, you know, when you start...' Mabby suddenly leaps off the floor like a cat and settles herself next to Bella stoking her hair. 'When you start going lala, I can't...'

'Yeah, I know, you can't think.' Bella lies down with her hands behind her head. Mabby lies down next to her weaving a rope of Bella's hair round her gnarled, brown finger.

'Well, that's what I have been doing. That's all there freakin' is to do in here. And I've been thinking about how you can get out of this black hole.'

Bella closes her eyes and resumes the story in her head while Mabby's bony hands start their nightly journey.

They were so rich they could eat banoffee pie for breakfast and sardines for supper and bathe every day in olive oil and cow's milk.

Bella tries to sit straight up in the stiff-backed chair and smile at the glass. The room on the other side is dark and she doesn't recognise the reflection of herself with the deep grey hollows where her eyes should be and her hair like rats' tails. She knows that somewhere someone is observing this and making notes. The door to the other room opens slowly, making the light flicker on automatically, and Mrs Bird, comes through looking puzzled. Bella tries to hide her disappointment that Joe isn't with her. Mrs Bird notices Bella and jumps like she's seen a ghost. Her mouth is a flat, straight line. She sits down looking uncomfortable and stares at Bella. She wonders if she can really see her. She is still wearing that same purple coat from the day of... the day when it all went wrong.

'Where's Joe?' she says too loud. Mrs Bird just stares, her mouth wriggling a bit at the ends but not opening. She is doing something under the table with her hands but Bella can't see what. Now it's Bella who squirms, wondering how to keep the fizzing in her legs from making her hands break something. They'll be watching. She has to keep still. She thinks about the bureau, a picture of swans on a lake. She breathes slowly, she tries to keep her voice even.

'Is Joe alright?' She watches Mrs Bird's face as it twists round her skull trying to keep her thoughts in her head. Bella imagines a thundercloud passing over the room, its shadow making them both shiver.

'Joe is not hurting anymore,' she says carefully enunciating the words as if each one was made of leaden toffee.

'But where is he? When can I see him? Why won't you bring him?' Bella jumps up at the window and presses herself against the cool glass. Mrs Bird flinches but gets up sedately, slowly turns round and leaves the room, plunging it in darkness as Bella slides to the floor.

'I hear you have been using story therapy.' Dr Jones peers at Bella, her eyes are not so twinkly today without the glasses. 'That can be very therapeutic.'

'Are you wearing contact lenses?' Bella notices the doctor isn't playing noughts and crosses today.

'Would you like to tell *me* the story in our session now?'

'I had banoffee pie this morning.' Bella smiles winningly. She hooks her hair behind both ears.

'I'd like to hear the one about Mabby.'

'I don't know any stories about Mabby.'

'We were thinking of assessing you for social association time. You have been in a single cell for three months.'

'When will I be able to see Joe?'

'Bella, we've talked about this a lot. You need to move on. Tell me the story about Mabby.'

'There isn't any story about Mabby. I want to see my son. It's Dan, isn't it? He's been writing to you again, hasn't he? Filling your head with lies about me.'

'Oh dear, I thought we had moved on from this one, Bella. Dan hasn't been writing to us.'

'He must have been!' Bella starts to clutch at her thighs. 'He must have. He always used to...'

'Bella, there is no record of anyone called Dan Jackson, or any of the details you have given about him. Your dissociative states are getting more frequent. It looks like we will have to carry on the treatment for another month then review it again.

'But there is! There is! It was in the papers! He broke in

during the night and got the carving knife out of the kitchen, he stabbed my wrists to make it look like I'd done myself in, then stabbed Joe fifteen times in his throat, his chest, his...

'Bella, stop, stop now.' Dr Jones leans forward slightly. 'Bella, stop.'

'That was you.'

THE LAST COIN

GEMMA ALLEN

"This is my last coin," she said, handing it over to the shopkeeper.

In return Jen was given a hot drink, which she clasped between her gloved hands. The material was already thinning and breaking, and not as protective as it should have been against the harshest of all winters.

Leaving the heated shop, she began to amble down the road. There was no destination, just a general movement in one direction in order to keep busy. Jen enjoyed stretching her legs, rather than sitting on the freezing pavement. She did that far too much.

Passing several friends on her way, she reached the park. There she sat on a bench, watching young children playing. It brought a smile to her face, even if it did remind her of her own. They would be home, warm and safe, with their dad. That was the important thing. Jen was used to the outside life by now, several years on.

The girl shrieked as she went high on the swing, pushed by an enthusiastic older boy.

"Stop, stop, I'm going to be sick!"

The boy laughed and pushed her again, even harder. Jen shook her head. Where were the parents? She made her way over to the children and addressed the boy sharply.

"Come on, can't you see she's scared?"

"What's it to you, old bag!"

He spat in Jen's face and she stepped back in shock. Normally the only people that spat on her were drunk and walking past her sleeping bag. This felt different. She felt vulnerable.

She summoned up all her courage and tried to speak with an even tone.

"Just stop it."

The boy shrugged and walked off. As the swing began to slow, Jen grabbed a hold of it. The girl leapt off and hugged her gratefully.

"Thank you, I was so scared."

"It's okay."

Jen hugged back, momentarily imagining her own daughter in her arms. The girl moved away, and Jen came back to the present.

"Thanks."

She skipped off, and Jen left the park. It was time to go home.

THROUGH THE LOOKING GLASS
KATH CROFT

I hang the mirror in the hall, a heavy, decorative thing. Ormolu. Gilded frame around the glass conceals a hidden depth. My face, old and worn, is reflected with great detail; the lines, the wrinkles all revealed. My youthful beauty is no more.

If I step aside, the mirror splits my face in two. A ripple hidden beneath its surface. It too is flawed; no longer young and clear, we both have had our day. I move my head back and forth as if in the arcade, where as a child I laughed as I shrank and grew.

Standing here, I remember it. Bought, from an auction house, where those who aspired to the grander things would come, 'just to see' the second-rate goods, sold off cheap. But Aunty didn't care what others bought, this grand mirror was her desire.

And now it's mine, hanging in my hall. Large, ugly, demanding I keep the secret, close to the wall. I move my head and now I see myself as I truly am. Bright and bubbly, young once more, my age slips away beneath the fold, hidden in the glass.

TROUBLES

OWEN TOWNEND

Craig grabbed a snug while Vernon was still gabbling at the bar.

"Help us out, son," he eventually spoke from the other side of the saloon door. Craig put down his phone and grabbed the old metal grip handle. Guinness spilled across Vernon's knuckle as he brought the pint glasses down onto the varnished wooden table. Craig fished around the ledge of the stained window for a beermat that wasn't flaking.

"I asked for a gin and tonic," he grumbled, fingers sticky from touching the sides of the glass.

"Did you?" Vernon frowned, regarding both drinks. He shrugged. "Still, when in Belfast, drink as the Irish do, eh?"

Craig lobbed a second soggy mat at Vernon as he shuffled along the opposing black leather seat. The older man tutted. "Get it down you then."

He watched Craig peer at it through his glasses then take an exploratory sip. Vernon wanted to see his stiff-collared son loosen up a little. And what a place for it.

"The Crown Liquor Saloon." Vernon whistled as he took in the pub, from the checkerboard tile floor up to the intricate dark brown swirls of the ceiling. "You know your grandfather almost brought me here once."

Craig wrinkled his nose. "When was this?"

"Late 60s."

"You missed it on account of the Troubles then?"

Vernon nodded. "We didn't hang around. Soon as his brother got back about a place in York, we were gone."

"So was granddad Protestant or Catholic?"

"Well, he was raised a Catholic but he changed his answer wherever he went in town. He knew how to get by." At last Vernon shrugged off his brown leather jacket. "You enjoying your pint?"

"More than you, it seems."

"I'll get to it. Honestly, what do you think?"

Craig held the glass up to regard the sloshing liquid inside. He pouted.

"Tastes better in Dublin."

Vernon glanced around them. "Careful what you say in here."

"It's fine. The booths around us are full of tourists."

"Still there are the local lads at the bar. The one who served me was halfway through some kind of joke about the Republic."

"And he went through with it?" For the first time since arriving a smile tweaked the left side of Craig's mouth. "What was the joke?"

Vernon finally tipped back his pint. "Local humour. Nothing I really understood." Bringing it back down again, he snapped his fingers and pointed to the far right of the bar by the front entrance. "You see that mirror?"

Craig had to get his knees up on the seat and cover his eyes from the glare of all the polished brass and glass surrounding the bar. He could just about spy a large curved decorative wall mirror in the corner.

"You see the crack?" Vernon asked.

Craig couldn't see much past two fast-talking businessmen who were gesticulating wildly with their hands.

"That's a bullet hole," Vernon continued. "One of the shots fired during the worst of the Troubles."

Craig raised an eyebrow. "Isn't this also the most bombed pub in the city?"

"Yes. They fixed all that up though. The bullet hole still remains as a mark of history." Vernon sank back more Guinness, eyes raised upward again. "Well, that and the roof."

Craig followed his gaze to the treacle-coloured spirals that dulled the yellow lighting of the bar. "That's thick with tar surely."

"Maybe." Vernon chuckled. "You can almost imagine the local lads smoking and drinking in here for hours on end, risking their lives for just a few laughs."

At last Craig picked up his own pint again. "Quite the risk when you think about it."

"Perhaps some of them found the risk of a bust-up preferable to staying at home with the wife." Vernon winked.

"Maybe," Craig replied, eyes downcast. "Some might even have decided not to go back."

He glanced to check the quiet hurt on Vernon's face. "What was that?"

"You heard me."

Rubbing his chin stubble, Craig's father sighed. "This was supposed to be a bonding trip, Craig."

"You mean the quality father-son time we didn't have the first go around?"

"I have apologised profusely. To your mother, to yourself, to damn near everyone."

Craig's eyes widened. "And you think that's enough?"

"It happened ten years ago." Vernon ran his fingers through his thinning hair. "I hurt your mother, I was a fool but I grovelled, I begged, I admitted I was wrong."

"Most people would do that last bit first."

Vernon folded his arms. This only brought out more indignance in his son.

"I was eight, Dad. Eight!" Craig glared at him. "You left! Mum and I were in pieces and you just...left."

Vernon breathed in and out slowly. Craig rolled his eyes. The hubbub of the bar rose up around them, belittling their silence. A dirty cackle burst out of a nearby toilet.

"Eight," Vernon muttered.

"Yeah."

"I was the same age when my dad ran."

Craig frowned.

"From here. From home."

"It's not the same, Dad."

Vernon nodded. "No two wreckages are ever the same. But they're still wreckage." He tried to catch his son's eye but Craig was focusing hard on the remaining foam on the rim of his glass. Vernon gave a tight smile. "But at least they put this place back together."

"National Trust can't mend everything." Craig placed the empty glass down on the beermat so hard that both rattled. He reached behind him and hit the bell.

Vernon stared at the lion sculpture that was looming over his son's head. Shoulders hunched, Craig seemed to shrink beneath it. Vernon was sure there was something he could say but it wouldn't come to him. Besides, between the Guinness and the low lighting, he was beginning to feel too sluggish for any further words. Weighed down by the atmosphere. Weighed by the Crown Liquor Saloon.

"Perhaps we should have just had this conversation in the hotel," he muttered. Craig said nothing. They waited some time for service.

WISH YOU WERE HERE

GARETH CLEGG

Through simple postcards
I feel places come alive
In all their beauty

White capped mountains rise
Gods of rock, they tower high
Above their subjects

Volcanic lava
Rivers of furious fire
None outrun its wrath

Beneath ocean blue
You swim with whales and dolphins
Precious air above

Blistering sunlight
Ancient stone amid bleak sand
Egyptian ruins

While dark forests sleep
Hidden under vibrant green
Northern lights above

A great tale unfolds
Reliving all your travels
Wish I was there too

ACKNOWLEDGEMENTS

Cover Design by
Sophie Alderheart, Gareth Clegg

Edited by
Owen Townend, Jenn Murg,
Vivien Teesdale, Gareth Clegg

HUDDERSFIELD AUTHORS' CIRCLE

Formed in 1935, the first president was James Richard Gregson, a writer and actor. Past presidents have included Hazel Wheeler, who wrote many books based on her life in Huddersfield. The presidency was, and still is, for one year only.

In addition to poetry, short stories and plays, many of the members had articles published in local papers or read on the radio. Meetings included speakers on a variety of topics, workshops and readings from members.

Both venues and format of meetings adapted to new members and new circumstances, but the advent of Covid changed everything considerably. Online sessions allowed the group to continue to meet, read and run modified workshops, though it is hoped to return to face-to-face meetings as soon as conditions allow.

Visit our website for more information:
HuddersfieldAuthorsCircle.co.uk

SOPHIE ALDERHEART

Full time Nerd, part-time barbarian;

Sophie first began writing at the age of 5 and has been hooked on books ever since. She joined HAC six years ago, and has loved spending her time amongst such talented writers who inspire who to take her writing above and beyond.

In her fiction, she likes to explore morality within big adventure, with a touch of human flaw.

SARA BURGESS

Sara Burgess is writing her third novel, a historical dual narrative observation of the most haunted house in England. Not a ghost story, it explores the fascinating characters in the life of what was once dubbed a red brick monstrosity.

Sara writes short stories and the odd poem and script. Fellow writers in HAC know her for her highly descriptive style. She has been a member of the group for almost two decades and has served as president twice. There may be the occasional inscription on a HAC trophy from past wins.

Sara is keen to get this novel published.... When it's finished!

GARETH CLEGG

Gareth is a professional editor and bestselling author based in Lepton, Huddersfield.

He specialises in Sci-Fi and Dark Fantasy stories with one steampunk novel Fogbound: Empire in Flames, and a Dark Fantasy Western novella series, Chronicles of the Fallen to his name along with several short stories in collections and anthologies.

Amazon Author Page: geni.us/garethclegg
Website: GarethClegg.com

amazon.com/author/garethclegg
facebook.com/GOcmdO
twitter.com/GOcmdO
goodreads.com/garethclegg

KATH CROFT

My name is Kath Croft and I have been a member of the 'Huddersfield Author's Circle' for many years and am best known for writing short stories, although I have recently written some poetry. I have had two stories published, one in a successful anthology called 'Sexy Shorts For Summer' in aid of 'Cancer Research' and the other in 'Scary Shorts For Halloween' in aid of the 'Breast Cancer Campaign'. Both published by Accent Press Ltd. One of these stories was then read by Paul Ross in his 'Big Black Book of Horror' on the 'Paranormal Chanel' produced by 'Antix productions' and was consequently featured in 'Charley Brooker's Screen Wipe' programme on the B.B.C.

I have been quite successful with my poetry, winning the open poetry competition in the Mrs Sunderland festival on one occasion and being placed second and third in other years.

SUSIE FIELD

I was born in Brighouse, West Yorkshire, but have lived in the village of Clifton for almost 50 years. I have been married for 52 years and have a son and daughter and three granddaughters.

I have been writing poetry and short stories for many years and am a member of Huddersfield Authors' Circle (HAC) and Rastrick Poets.

Many of my poems have been published in the Huddersfield Examiner and Yorkshire Post, and I have also had six books published in total. My last two publications, Step Into the Unknown and A Moment in Time, have been charity books supporting Leeds Spinal Surgery Support Fund. Both these books are available on Amazon and through the HAC website, or by e-mailing me direct at bellfield2@sky.com

Susie Field

NICK STEAD

A lifelong fan of supernatural horror and fantasy, Nick spends his days prowling the darker side of fiction, often to the scream of heavy metal guitars and the purrs of his feline companions.

Nick is best known for his Hybrid series. He has also had short stories published in various anthologies, and will soon be releasing his first non-Hybrid novel based on the true story of the Pendle witches.

For more information visit: **www.nick-stead.co.uk**. Don't forget to sign up to his newsletter to keep up to date with upcoming releases and signing events, and receive a free short story, exclusive to the mailing list.

To receive notification direct from Amazon, simply click the Follow button on his Amazon Author Page to be informed when new books are out. **Author.to/nickstead**

Or check out his Goodreads page:
goodreads.com/author/show/14138888.Nick_Stead

He's also on social media:

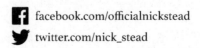

facebook.com/officialnickstead
twitter.com/nick_stead

VIVIEN TEASDALE

Though I've always written, even before I knew how to form the letters properly, it was a love of crime (writing, not perpetrating) and history that brought me to my first serious writing, for Wharncliffe Pen & Sword books – all available through their website:

https://www.pen-and-sword.co.uk/search/author/Vivien+Teasdale

Besides family history, to local and social history, my writing also includes poetry and short stories, having twice won short story competitions in Writers' News magazine, as well as a number of our HAC competitions.

I've also turned my hand to novels and have the beginnings of a series of crime stories.

One day I will finish these, but at the moment I'm far too engrossed in a fantasy world which, one way or another, I have to save from complete destruction.

OWEN TOWNEND

Owen Townend is a Huddersfield-born writer of short speculative fiction and has been published by Comma Press, Arachne Press, and Twisted Fate Publishing among others.

He is currently working on a trilogy of Western novellas. As of writing this bio, Owen has been a member of HAC for 6 years.

Blog
http://mrpondersome.blogspot.com/?m=1

Twitter
@mrpondersome

Printed in Great Britain
by Amazon